The Kinley Legacy

From business to forever!

The Kinley company has been the prestige brand in British fashion for more than a century, but a series of bad investments has left the coffers nearly bare and the company in need of a miracle.

Now, to right the wrongs of their parents and save the Kinley name and legacy, the estranged Kinley siblings—Jonathan, Olivia and Caleb—will have to set aside their differences to come together and show the world what "family" really means.

Escape to the Cotswolds in Jonathan's story:
Reunion with the Brooding Millionaire

Follow Olivia's story in London and Paris:
Rules of Their Parisian Fling

Embark on a vacation to Lake Como in Caleb's story:
The Millionaire's Italian Invitation

All available now!

Dear Reader,

Welcome to the final installment of The Kinley Legacy. If you've been here since the start, THANK YOU from the bottom of my heart for being with me on this journey. If you're only just discovering this world, WELCOME! I'm so glad to have you here.

Writing these stories has been an absolute joy and wouldn't have been possible without all the wonderful people cheering from the sidelines. I owe every single one of you a huge debt of gratitude.

I hope you fall for Caleb and Ally just as hard as I did.

Love,

Ellie Darkins

x

The Millionaire's Italian Invitation

Ellie Darkins

Recycling programs
for this product may
not exist in your area.

ISBN-13: 978-1-335-73681-9

The Millionaire's Italian Invitation

Copyright © 2022 by Ellie Darkins

For questions and comments about the quality of this book,
please contact us at CustomerService@Harlequin.com.

Harlequin Enterprises ULC
22 Adelaide St. West, 41st Floor
Toronto, Ontario M5H 4E3, Canada
www.Harlequin.com

Printed in U.S.A.

Ellie Darkins spent her formative years devouring romance novels and, after completing her English degree, decided to make a living from her love of books. As a writer and editor, she finds her work now entails dreaming up romantic proposals, hot dates with alpha males and trips to the past with dashing heroes. When she's not working, she can usually be found running around after her toddler, volunteering at her local library or escaping all the above with a good book and a vanilla latte.

Books by Ellie Darkins

Harlequin Romance

Holiday with the Mystery Italian
Falling for the Rebel Princess
Conveniently Engaged to the Boss
Surprise Baby for the Heir
Falling Again for Her Island Fling
Reunited by the Tycoon's Twins
Snowbound at the Manor
From Best Friend to Fiancée
Prince's Christmas Baby Surprise
Reunion with the Brooding Millionaire
Rules of Their Parisian Fling

Visit the Author Profile page at Harlequin.com.

For all my readers

Praise for
Ellie Darkins

PROLOGUE

Ally: You're never going to believe what my parents have done now!

Caleb: IDK? Smothered you with love and affection?

Well… Yes. Obviously. But you're going to have to be more specific if you want to win the speedboat.

I already have a speedboat.

What? Really?! Of course you do…

Stop stalling.

Guess!

They… I don't know…made you dinner?

Caleb, that's not smothering. That's normal parenting.

Maybe for people whose parents didn't send them to boarding school and then leave the country…

embarrassed emoji Sorry, sorry. We don't have to play. You already have a speedboat!

It's fine. I was teasing. I want the boat. They… set you up on a date again? Even though you begged them not to after you broke that nice doctor's heart?

I did *not* break his heart!

But was I right?

Sort of… Except it's much worse. Hang on… Need to copy and paste:

Dear Ally, Welcome to the Single No More family! We can't wait to welcome you on board for a trip of a lifetime. A cruise around the beautiful Scilly Isles with other vetted and background-checked singles. Prepare for romantic candlelit dinners, evening strolls around the decks and days relaxing by the pool…

There's more, but you get the idea.

Ally…is this…real? Do they really want you to go?

Yes. I need to get out of it. Any ideas? Also, how's the wedding going?

Excruciating. Rowan and Jonathan are besotted. Adam and Liv are barely keeping their hands to themselves. They glare at me every time I pick up my phone. How early is too early to leave?

You have to stay until they cut the cake. You can do it. I believe in you.

Easy for you to say. Can't believe I have to go to Italy with them in a week. A whole seven days of family time. If you figure out the answer to getting out of awkward family stuff…

Cal?

…

CAL!

…

Cal, are you there?

Hey, Liv confiscated my phone. Have you packed for your cruise yet?

Don't laugh, please? I have to get out of this.

Can't you just tell them you don't want to go?

Tried it. Didn't take. So I did something that you're probably going to be mad about…

What did you do?

I told Mum I had a boyfriend.

You said you'd already tried that?

I did. She didn't believe me. Wanted to know

who it was. Because apparently the only person I ever talk about is you. So I told her it was you. My boyfriend. I told her you were my boyfriend…

…

Cal? You still there?

CHAPTER ONE

THIS WAS FINE. He was fine, Ally was fine, and everything between him and Ally was fine.

There was absolutely no reason that he should be freaking out about the fact that her lying to her parents about them dating had somehow snowballed in the space of a week to him standing at the arrivals gate at Bari airport, waiting to meet his best friend in person for the first time. And then trying to convince his own family as well as hers that they were dating for real and didn't need any further interference in their love lives—or lack thereof.

Caleb remembered how inspired he had felt when the solution to both their problems had struck him as he'd read Ally's last message in the middle of the night. She'd needed to convince her parents to stop trying to find her a boyfriend. He could convince his siblings that he was perfectly happy with the life that he was living, and they could stop worrying about him and covertly staring at him between sessions of making out with their new partners in places that were way too public for his liking.

They had gone from subtly criticising the amount of time that he spent staring at a screen to full-on confiscating his devices. Somehow, his protestations that he was both working and talking to his friend hadn't been enough to convince them that he was capable of making his own choices about living his life and that they didn't have to worry about him any more. Perhaps they would be more understanding if they thought that he was sexting...

He'd been facing the prospect of a week of poolside 'family time'—because somehow his brother and new sister-in-law, his sister and her boyfriend, had decided to crash his annual visit to the Italian villa that he had inherited from their grandparents—and if he didn't want them to worry about him he was going to have to occasionally put down his phone and his laptop and spend time with them.

And what better way to convince them that he was *'absolutely fine, thanks'* than by introducing them to the person that he had been spending all his time hanging out with—online—over the last year.

Instead of being dragged away by his family when all he really wanted to do was chat with Ally, he could just…invite Ally along. That way he wouldn't have to justify the time that he wanted to spend talking to her. All that plotting and scheming aside, he'd love for her to come to Italy, for her own sake. For his. Because after all this time putting it off, the thought of actually spending a week with his best friend without a screen between them felt like too much of a treat to pass up.

They'd put this off—the meeting in person thing—for so long that he'd started to forget that it wasn't the way that friendships normally worked. They lived in the same city. They could have jumped in an Uber and spent time together in the real world any time in the past year.

They'd met on an online role-playing

game, started chatting as they'd played. When they'd realised that they'd spent more time chatting than playing, they'd moved their friendship off the platform and for the past few months had spent most of their days messaging one another with something that they thought would make the other laugh. The details of their day. Offloading about their families when it all became too much.

They could have just met for a coffee in London, where they both lived. That would have made so much more sense than doing this here, in a foreign airport, with his whole family waiting for him at the end of their short drive home.

But things had got to the point where they had gone so long with neither of them suggesting a coffee that the thought of doing it had become this big, insurmountable obstacle in their way. Ally's friendship had become so important to him that he didn't want to do anything that might risk her deciding that he really wasn't worth the effort. So rather than tackle that obstacle, he'd let the pressure build up behind it until— *poof*—he was issuing invitations for a week in Italy with his family halfway through his brother's wedding rather than suggesting an Americano in his local coffee shop.

The problem with wanting to get close to Ally was that…well, he knew what happened when someone got close to her—like that doctor who was absolutely not good enough for her. They got shown the door before they could get too comfortable. And he'd seen what happened when people got close to him—his parents had felt so burdened by their children that they'd upped and left them without a backward glance before he was even out of school. And Jonathan had inherited the responsibility for a teenager and had never quite managed to hide how much it had cost him.

If Caleb keeping his friendship with Ally solely online was what kept it alive, he'd been okay with that. But this… If they could do this without Ally getting freaked out and bailing on their friendship, without him feeling as though he was a burden to everyone who cared about him, they could hang out for a week to get their families off their backs, and then they could go back to hanging out online, as they had for the last year.

So why were his palms sweating?

It was just because the aircon in the terminal building was non-existent and Ally's plane was late, so he'd been standing in the heat waiting for her for two hours. Probably his siblings still thought that Ally was going to turn out to be a figment of his imagination and stage another of those 'don't you think you should put down your devices' interventions. It wasn't as if he didn't leave the house—he spent time outdoors, he travelled, he explored London. But he wasn't exactly going to invite his family along when they'd just spend the whole time feeling as though they were responsible for him or something. And these days he preferred to have his phone or his laptop with him so that he could chat to Ally while he was doing it.

It didn't seem to matter how many times that he told his family that he had everything he needed, friends and a social life included, they continued to worry. He wasn't sure how much time a week pretending to date Ally would buy him, but he was willing to take what he could get.

When another stream of people began to pass through the arrivals gate, he watched as couples and families and lone travellers emerged from the corridor without any sign of Ally.

The stream of people petered out and he was resigning himself to waiting even longer when he saw her. She had her eyes on her phone screen, brows drawn together in concentration. She dragged behind her a shiny silver suitcase, and wore a bright orange sundress, almost the same colour as her hair, which had slipped a little to reveal a creamy-white shoulder and the strap of a halter neck bikini. She was going to burn in this heat, he thought. At that moment, she looked up, caught his gaze on her, and a smile spread from her wide mouth, up over rosy apple cheeks to sparkling dark eyes. She stopped in front of him without a shred of uncertainty.

'Ally?' he asked. She replied by wrapping her arms around his neck, squeezing tight and squealing in his ear.

'Caleb! I can't believe it's you.'

'You barely even checked.' He laughed, holding her at arm's length to get a proper look at her. She was…amazing. Bright colours and tumbling curly hair and curves everywhere, so tempting to the eye that he drew his eyes swiftly away and fixed them on her face instead, where he thought they would be safer. He was wrong, because she looked knowingly at him and laughed. 'What if you'd got the wrong guy?'

'Of course it was you. You look... I don't know. Just like you. Have you been waiting long?' she asked. He dodged the question and reached for Ally's suitcase before she snatched it out of reach and pulled it along as they headed for the enormous sliding doors out of the terminal building. 'How long will it take us to drive to your place?' Ally asked as they climbed into the car.

'About half an hour until my family embarrass me completely and you regret ever agreeing to this,' Caleb told her, only half joking.

'Come on, they can't be as bad as mine. So, what have you told them?' she asked as they pulled out of the airport car park and narrowly avoided being swiped by a dinged-up Fiat that seemed to have come out of nowhere.

'About what?' he asked, flicking on his indicator and gritting his teeth as he approached a roundabout. He'd only arrived in Italy yesterday and hadn't quite acclimatised to the local driving yet.

Ally whacked his arm once they were on the road towards the villa.

'So have you told them *anything* about who I am and why I'm here and everything like that?'

He glanced across at her before focusing his eyes safely back on the road.

'I told them that I was bringing someone.'

She rolled her eyes. 'That's it? You didn't tell them that we're friends or how we met or that I lied to my parents and told them we were dating?'

He shrugged again, pulling out to overtake a slower car in front. 'I didn't want to overstep. We haven't really talked about what's going on and I wasn't sure whether the pretending to be your boyfriend was just for your family or mine too.' And even without that complication, he wouldn't know how to explain their friendship to the others in a way that they would understand. It was only occurring to him now—in a way that made him realise how seriously he had had his head in the sand about this—that it would have made much more sense to discuss this before Ally had actually arrived.

He didn't trust that his family would understand that Ally could be his best friend despite the fact that they hadn't met in person before this weekend. If he'd thought about it he would probably have guessed that if he turned up with a woman that they'd not met before, then his family would assume that she was his girlfriend. But perhaps that was why he'd tried so hard *not* to think about it—had he wanted them to jump to that conclusion? What would that mean for his friendship with Ally, his feelings about her?

'Well, I told my parents you were my boyfriend,' Ally observed wryly, her eyes fixed firmly on the landscape ahead of them. 'I probably overstepped for the both of us.'

He risked a glance across at her as he pulled out onto the highway. 'If it helps, my family will probably just assume that we're together,' he told her, trying to keep his voice safely neutral.

'And you're okay with that?' Ally asked.

He took a deep breath. 'I think it will stop them bugging me about whether I have a girlfriend and shouldn't I go out more and is it healthy for me to spend so much of my time working. For some reason they worry about me, and I don't want them to. You'll be doing me a favour if we go along with it. They'd probably just ask more questions if I told them that we're only friends.'

He was aware of her looking at him for a few moments before she spoke again. 'Well, okay. As long as we have our stories straight about this before I meet everyone.'

That surprised a laugh out of Caleb, an uncanny reminder that this was the same woman who made him laugh on a daily basis, only this was the first time that she was around to hear it. 'Ally, we didn't rob a bank. We don't need to *"get our stories straight"*. It's none of their business what we are to each other.'

'Of course it's not, but I don't want to get caught out! I told my family that you were my boyfriend and that you're whisking me away to your holiday home. They're going to want pictures or they'll think I'm making it up. And we can't just say *nothing* to your family. It'll be embarrassing, for one thing, and make them think you're weirder than they already do, for another.'

Caleb snorted another laugh. 'Well, thank you for that vote of confidence. Fine. We'll tell them that you're my girlfriend. They're always telling me that they're worried I spend so much time working or looking at a screen. It never seems to matter how many times I tell them that I don't want them to worry about me. I don't want that happening again, and if it takes a little white lie to make it go away then I'm okay with that.'

Ally gave him a look that was a little too searching to be comfortable. 'I'm not saying that I agree with them,' she said gently. 'And you don't have to lie to your family. I'm happy being your friend, Cal. I just don't want to walk in there unprepared.'

But Caleb shook his head. Because this was the perfect solution. If he turned up with Ally as his girlfriend, there would be no more worrying about him. No more interventions. No more feeling as if his very presence in their lives was a burden that they'd inherited and did not deserve. 'No, this is good. This is a good plan. So, where did we meet?'

'We met playing an online computer game,' Ally said. 'I think that we should stick to the truth whenever we can. Looking like we're overthinking it is going to be the biggest giveaway.'

'And now we're dating.' He looked across at her, suddenly panicked. 'I mean, that's what we'll tell them. I know that we're not.'

'Okay,' Ally said, and he didn't think he could bear to look over at her and try and see what she was thinking. 'Fine. So we met online. Then what?'

'I don't know,' Caleb said, thinking out loud. 'We started talking, decided to meet up as we both lived in London and hit it off. Most of that's true except for the meeting up part.'

'I suppose it sounds plausible enough,' Ally said. 'And then we started dating? How long ago?'

'Six months?' he threw out, trying to remember when chatting to Ally had become something that had become so much a fixture of his day that he couldn't remember what life had been like before.

'Fine,' Ally agreed. 'We've been dating

for six months. Which side of the bed do you sleep on?'

Caleb's eyebrows flew up to somewhere near his hairline. 'Ally, we don't have to... I mean, we have a spare room and—'

She shook her head, hoping that the movement would hide the pink she was sure was staining her cheeks. 'I only meant in case someone asks. That's the sort of thing that we should know about each other.'

He reached over and covered her hand with his, feeling the slight shake there that would have given away that she was nervous even if he hadn't already guessed.

'Ally, no one is going to ask us which side of the bed we sleep on. And if you don't want to share a bed, or a room, that's fine; we have plenty of space.'

'We're hardly going to be convincing as a couple if we don't sleep together,' she pointed out.

Caleb shook his head. 'You seem to think that I care a lot more about my brother and sister figuring this out than I do about what you want. That couldn't be further from the truth. I want you to be comfortable here. I want this arrangement to work for you without you having to do *any*thing that makes you uncomfortable. If sharing a room is too weird, then we won't do it. It's that simple.'

'What would you prefer?' Ally asked.

'I'd…prefer that we share. A room, at least. Just because that way it's easier for us to hang out in there away from the others. We don't have to share the bed, if you don't want. I can sleep on the couch.'

'Did it occur to you that it might be fun to hang out *with* your family?'

He laughed. 'Give it a day and you'll be rethinking that notion. Trust me.'

'What's so terrible about them?' Ally asked, because in all the time that she'd known Caleb, he'd barely spoken about his family other than that he was generally just frustrated with them.

'Honestly,' he told her, rubbing at his hair. 'I can't believe I used to get annoyed with Liv and Jonathan for fighting. Now Jonathan, my brother, is married to Liv's best friend—that's Rowan. And then Liv—my sister—moved in with Adam, who she and Jonathan work with. Since they all coupled up they're terribly earnest and smug and settled and won't be happy until I'm making the same life choices as they are. They worry about me constantly and nothing I say or do seems to be able to convince them to stop. It drives me up the wall.'

'I can see why that would be annoying,' Ally said diplomatically. 'What are these life choices they object to?' she asked. 'You look like you're doing okay to me.' She smiled, and he only just resisted the urge to sell his soul to whoever would buy it in order to see that again.

'They seem to think that the only way I can possibly be happy is if I have a partner. I don't think that spending my time with my favourite person will count in their eyes if it's a friend that I met online.'

'In that case isn't spending more time with me going to add to the problem rather than solve it?' she asked.

He kept his eyes on the road, tried to keep his voice neutral. 'Hence the boyfriend charade.'

'Because spending your life talking to me is questionable, but having sex with me is okay?' He could feel his cheeks heat and hoped she would blame it on the sun. Because he really, really couldn't handle her talking about sex right now, when he was only just getting used to the fact that she was an actual real-life person sitting less than a metre away. Someone who he could just reach out and *touch*.

'It's their logic, not mine. I'm not saying that I understand it. Personally, I'm just really pleased that I get to hang out with you for the week.' This time when she looked across at her she was looking at him intently.

'What?' he asked.

'Just checking, but we are just *pretending* to be sleeping together?' she said, and he got the impression that she was weighing her words carefully. It took every ounce of concentration he had to keep the car on the road when his every instinct was to swerve to the verge, get a proper look at her and try and work out whether she was saying that because she wanted... No. No thinking about wanting. Only thinking about driving.

'Of course we're just pretending,' he said, still not daring to look at her.

'Okay, well, no need to be quite so vehement,' Ally said with a thin laugh. 'I'll have you know that some people enjoy having sex with me.'

He wasn't sure that he could blush any harder, but at the same time was sure that with every word that left her mouth he was managing to reach unsurpassed levels of pinkness. 'I don't doubt that,' he said honestly. 'But it is probably the sort of thing that I would ask before you arrived in a different country to hang out with me.'

'Well, yes, I'd have hoped so too,' Ally said with a laugh. 'But it doesn't do any harm to check.'

Thankfully she dropped the subject after that and he managed to keep the car on the road all the way back to the villa, where he clicked the remote to open the gates, and took the opportunity to look at Ally properly for the first time since they had got in the car.

'Is there anything else we need to cover before we meet people?' Ally asked as the gates of the villa came into view. 'Like are we dating other people?'

He shook his head, stifled a laugh. 'I'm impressed you think I would pull that off in the week that we're here.'

'I meant that if we've been together six months, are there other people we need to explain away.' She shifted in her seat so that she could look at him properly. He put the handbrake on so that he could do the same, because for some reason it felt important to get this right.

'No. I... I've not dated anyone that recently,' he said carefully.

'Okay, well. Me neither. So we don't need to worry about that one.'

A silence lingered, though Caleb couldn't see why. It didn't mean anything that they hadn't been dating anyone recently. That was the whole reason that they were here. And the fact that it coincided with how long they'd been friends? Well, it was just that—coincidence.

It seemed unbelievable to him now that they'd managed to maintain a friendship for more than a year without meeting in person, and yet she was somehow completely familiar. Crazy that she had had that face and that hair and that body and that *glow* all along, and he simply hadn't seen it before. She was bright and warm and just so completely *Ally* that now he'd met her he couldn't imagine her looking any other way.

What he hadn't been prepared for was

how he was going to feel when he saw her for the first time. A combination of, *Of course this is her,* and, *She's amazing,* and, *Well, of course I think she's amazing—she's my best friend so that shouldn't be a surprise,* and, *Oh, my God, I really want to kiss her.*

It was only the last one that was a problem, and that made him stall the car as he went to drive through the open gates. Ally raised her eyebrows at him.

'Everything okay?' she asked.

'Yeah, cool, fine, okay,' he gabbled, restarting the car and driving through the gateway into the driveway at the front of the villa. That was bad, the wanting to kiss her, wasn't it? It was just a weird reaction to meeting her in person finally, he told himself, trying to justify the feeling.

It was just the physicality of her that was messing with his brain. It wasn't, like, a crush. He couldn't really want to kiss her, could he? Because wanting to kiss her could lead to wanting other things, and he knew that he couldn't want that. All his own issues aside, he knew what happened to people who wanted Ally too much—she made sure that they didn't have a place in her life. And as much as he might have been blown away by meeting her in person for the first time, he couldn't imagine a future that didn't have her in it. As a friend. Just a friend, because that was the only way that Ally kept people in her life, and he would never ask more of her than she wanted to give. The only problem with those very sensible reasons why he should not want to kiss her was that he really, really did want to kiss her.

He opened the boot of the car and concentrated on getting Ally's bags out. He would just ignore this feeling, he told himself sternly. There was nothing else to do. He had invited her to stay with him as his friend and he wasn't going to change that. The novelty and strangeness of her actually being here would wear off and they would be who they always were to each other. And what was that?

Well, she was his best friend. She was the person that he wanted to speak to first in the morning. The one he had to text when his family were driving him round the bend, the person he wanted to hang out with more than any other.

Kissing could only ever make that more complicated. He wouldn't burden her with these feelings. Not when that risked pushing her away. They would pass—he was sure of it.

Ally was the best and most uncomplicated part of his life and there was no way that he was going to ask more of their friendship than he already had. It was what he lived in fear of—asking more of people than they wanted to give. Once his parents had farmed him out to boarding school and then left the country entirely, he'd taken the not so subtle hint that he really shouldn't expect too much of other people. It saved him from inevitable disappointment in the long run. And he'd already had more from Ally than he'd expected. He'd been lulled into a false sense of security getting to know her in a space he normally used to cut himself off from people. He should have guessed that meeting her in person would complicate things. He just had to remember that nothing had to change. Nothing had changed—all he had to do was make sure that things stayed that way all week.

'Come on, let me show you around,' he

said, putting on a smile that didn't quite feel natural. He could hear the others were by the pool, so he dropped the case by the front door and led Ally towards the corner of the house. The feel of Ally's hand in his drew him up short before they reached it. He had not been prepared for the flush of happiness, anticipation, *desire*, that the simple touch had inspired in him.

She widened her eyes at him in surprise.

'What, is this not okay? I just thought that if we're meeting everyone, we want to make it look like we're...'

Of course. That was why she had done it, because they were playing make-believe. He took a deep breath, fought down the waves of emotions that had just surged out of no-where and reminded his body that this was all fake. He couldn't read anything into her holding his hand.

'No, it's fine,' he said, giving her another smile that he hoped didn't look too forced. 'I just wasn't expecting it, that's all.' She went to pull her hand away, but he tightened his hand around hers before he lost hold of her.

'Are you really sure you want to go through with the fake boyfriend thing?'

she asked. 'Because we could just hang out this week,' she offered, looking at him as if she couldn't trust what he was thinking. 'We don't have to pretend we're something we're not.'

Well, that was enough of a reminder to bring him crashing back to reality. 'No, I'm sure. It's what the others need to hear to stop worrying about me. I just need a minute to get my head around it.'

'Around holding hands?' she asked, her brows drawing together.

'Around all of it,' he said, wondering how he could explain how he was feeling without giving away that he had been feeling way too much ever since he had collected her from the airport. 'I've never faked having a girlfriend around my family before,' he explained, knowing that that wasn't the half of what was going on.

'Maybe we're not the holding hands sort of couple?' she asked tentatively.

'No, I like this,' Caleb said, giving her fingers a squeeze. Realising too late that he was probably giving away too much.

But Ally didn't flinch, she just smiled at him. 'And what about the rest of it?' she asked. 'Do you normally go in for PDAs? Kissing in public?'

Caleb forced himself to take a deep breath, liking the idea of that a little too much. 'Well, I suppose it depends on the kiss,' he said, not able to resist the smile that accompanied his words. He looked her in the eyes for a few moments longer, and then leaned in.

Ally caught the scent of peppermint on his breath as his lips brushed across her cheekbone so lightly that she could barely feel it.

'That sort of thing would be fine,' he said.

She rolled her eyes. 'Yes, for an elderly relative. I was thinking more along the lines of…'

She paused, considering, and then stretched up on her tiptoes, let her top lip come to meet his, the barest hint of a kiss, a temptation to something more before she thought better of it and pulled away.

'If we're looking for the line, I think we're still a way short of it,' Caleb observed, his voice tight. 'That was barely a kiss at all.'

'Well, I'm sorry to have disappointed you. Maybe we're one of those couples who barely acknowledge each other in public. Or kiss on the cheek like they're in a marriage that has been dying for years.'

Caleb fought down a smile at that, but couldn't hide the way that his hands came to rest on her hips.

Ally shrugged, but still looked at him as if he wasn't making sense. 'Well, just act like you do when you bring a real girlfriend home to meet them,' she suggested. And then asked, 'What?' at the expression on his face.

'I've never brought a girl home before,' he explained. 'No one was serious enough.'

Ally stared at him for a too-revealing moment. 'Okay, well, I'm honoured to be the fake first girlfriend you introduce to your family,' she said carefully, because she hadn't realised how big a deal this was for him. He'd never brought anyone home before. That made this a big deal, right? Even if she was a fake girlfriend, she was a real friend, and it still meant something that he trusted her enough to bring her into his life like this.

She squeezed his hand. Her support was genuine even if their relationship wasn't. 'You sure the hand holding is okay?' she checked, and Caleb wasn't sure that anything had ever made him feel less manly than that check-in.

'Of course I'm sure,' he told her, trying to make himself believe it at the same time. 'I guess we're going to have to do more than that if we're going to make this look convincing.'

'You know, you could do a girl a favour and look less horrified at that thought.'

'I'm not horrified. I promise. Just realising that I hadn't really thought this through. But it's only a week and then everything can go back to normal.'

CHAPTER TWO

AND THEN EVERYTHING could go back to normal, as if he hadn't just looked at her as if he wanted to eat her up, and then the way his face had fallen as if he hated himself for thinking it.

She hadn't been prepared for Caleb in real life. She'd searched online for him once, curious about the man she was spending so much of her life talking to. She hadn't looked at the tabloid coverage of his parents' well-publicised tax irregularities and their subsequent flit to South America. She didn't need to know anything about that that he hadn't chosen to share with her. She had seen that the family business had enjoyed a lot of success recently, the release of a fragrance from their archives having apparently taken the fashion and beauty worlds by storm.

But she hadn't wanted to dig beyond that. She'd simply been curious to put a face to the name that spent so much time in her notifications bar. He was cute. She'd known that from his profile picture on social media. But it turned out there was a world of difference between seeing that face on her phone screen and seeing it in real life, where it came with a whole adorable range of facial expressions that matched his personality so perfectly that she actually had to remind herself that this was the first time she'd properly met him.

They just had to get this first meeting with his family out of the way and then they could hang with a game or a movie or just drink and talk as they did most nights. The only difference would be that she actually got to see the expression on his face when she beat him as she usually did.

He kept a tight hold of her hand as they walked around to the back of the villa, if that was the right word for a place like this. She thought that 'palace' might have been more appropriate. She felt an unaccustomed stab of nerves at the thought of meeting Caleb's family. But there was no need for that, she told herself sternly. For a start, she wasn't prone to people-pleasing. And, more important than that, she wasn't really Caleb's girlfriend so it didn't matter whether they liked her or not, as long as she could get them to stop worrying Caleb or thinking that there was anything wrong with the way that he was living his life and use this holiday to stop her parents trying to force her to have the sort of relationship that they had relied on for so long but she was certain could never make her happy.

She saw how much her parents loved her. How could she miss the way that they watched her, as if they still didn't believe that she had made it so far? Childhood leukaemia had taken the lives of so many of the kids who had become her friends in hospital, it was as if they still couldn't believe that they were the lucky ones who had got to take her home.

She'd seen enough grief and loss in her childhood to know what it would do to her parents to lose her. Why would she let anyone else love her as much as they did? Knowing how much loving her could destroy someone's future, she wasn't going to invite anyone else to do that.

The thought of being the centre of someone's world again like that chilled her. Sure, it might be a nice thing for some people, having the eyes of the person or people who loved you more than anyone in the world looking at you as if they couldn't drink in enough of you. As if they wanted to burn the image of you onto their retinas. But generally, that sort of thing was usually associated with positive experiences. Fixing the image of you in their mind for the sheer pleasure of seeing you. Not because they were taking a mental photograph to cling onto once you'd gone.

Any time anyone had looked at her like that since, she'd been able to feel it again— the fact that no one expected her to be here in a year's time. That every moment with her loved ones was tinged with sadness— they were mourning her before she was even gone. Her not dying hadn't cured that feeling. Couldn't un-taint those memories. The association between love and sadness.

Unfortunately, she couldn't make her parents understand that. Now that she'd made it to adulthood, they wanted her to have all the things that they'd dreamed of for their little girl when they were nursing her through yet another round of chemo. The big wedding, the perfect grandchildren. The idea that Ally might want something different was something they just didn't seem able to accept, no matter how many times she'd explained it to them. If this little white lie would stop them worrying, as well as interfering, that could only be a good thing.

She shook off the mood, remembering that she had a part to play. This week wasn't just for her. It was for Caleb.

She heard his family before she saw them, the relaxed laughs of people on holiday from their troubles with loved ones who were familiar and close and safe. There was an ease to their laughter and voices that was notably absent from the man who now had her fingers in a death grip. It was just starting to dawn on her that she had absolutely no idea what she was getting into here.

She'd focused so much of her energy working out how to escape the unhelpful dynamics of her own family, she hadn't really considered that she was walking straight into someone else's, and that might be just as uncomfortable, albeit in a novel way.

'We'll make this quick,' she promised him, feeling his body tense up the closer that they got to the other. Squeezing his hand as best she could, given that he was close to breaking her fingers. 'I've got you,' she added on instinct, sensing that he needed to hear it.

The strangeness of having known him for a year, and also for less than an hour, kept taking her by surprise. Sometimes he was just Caleb, her best friend who she fired off messages to at all hours of the day without giving it a thought. And sometimes he was the guy who was so much more attractive in real life than she had been expecting, which was going to make this week more confusing than she'd bargained for.

No. There was no need to make a big deal of this, she told herself. They both knew what they were to each other. They'd just agreed it all. They were best friends doing each other a favour. After this week they could just go back to how things were before. They'd both been entirely happy with that. This week was a temporary blip, rather than a fundamental change to their relationship. Friendship. Frelationship?

But this was so not the time to be thinking about this. She had his family to meet and convince that they didn't need to worry about Caleb—or whatever it was that they were doing that made him feel as if he needed a fake girlfriend for a family holiday. And they could also send happy holiday snaps to her family and that would be the end of it.

They rounded the corner of the villa onto an expansive terrace with an infinity pool, and a view out to the lake beyond. There were four people around the pool, in various states of dress and swimwear, all of them sun-kissed and wet-haired. Two women lay back on sun loungers, the tiny one in a bikini, the taller woman in running gear, while the men were chatting and pouring beers at a table between two of the loungers.

'Caleb's here!' the smaller of the two women shouted, and all of a sudden all four sets of eyes were on them, sunglasses being pulled off and both women sitting up on their loungers and interrogating her with their eyes. At least she had the decades of practice of her parents scrutinising her every time that she saw them. They tried to hide what they were doing, of course, but she knew all the same. They were making sure that she was whole, well. That there were no telltale signs on her skin or in her eyes of some invading cells returning to steal their little girl from them after they had fought so hard to keep her.

And she still saw the fear on their faces, that even fifteen years of good health hadn't been able to dispel. That one of these days the overwhelming good luck that had saved her from the clutches of leukaemia would run out and their worst fears would come true.

It was the reason she had a fake boyfriend and not a real one—she was self-aware enough to know that. Because she'd seen what loving her did to a person, and she wasn't going to invite anyone into her life to play the Russian roulette that her parents had been dealing with ever since she had been ill.

But the expressions on Caleb's family's faces were variations on simple, naked curiosity.

'Um, hi?' she said, offering a half-wave, trying to hide her discomfort.

The two women jumped up and came over to say hello and introduce themselves, and she found herself shaking hands with Caleb's brother and sister and their partners, who looked exactly as obsessed with each other as Caleb had said they were, but a whole lot friendlier.

Not that that seemed to be helping with Caleb, who was stiff and awkward by her side. His siblings' polite interest in her seemed to be making him more tense rather than less, and she tried to surreptitiously work out what he needed, the more silent he became. She answered his family's questions as best she could, but neither her heart nor her head were in the game. All she could think about was getting him away from a situation that so clearly made him uncomfortable. She looked up at him, trying to tell him with her eyes that he could pull the plug and get them out of there, but they hadn't had enough time together for her unspoken communication to work. And Caleb wasn't putting himself out of his own misery, so that decided it. She was pulling the plug.

He jumped as she put her arm around his waist, and she hoped that his family hadn't seen.

'I'm sorry to be really rude,' she said, 'but I'm absolutely knackered after my flight. Cal, do you mind if I crash out for a bit?' Her words seemed to jolt Caleb out of his frozen state because his arm came around her shoulder, pulling her closer into his side as he spoke.

'Ally, I'm sorry, I wasn't thinking. Yeah, I'll show you inside. Let's go.'

She had to fight not to show her reaction to Caleb's hand landing on her shoulder. She shouldn't have flinched, she told herself. If they were really together the touch of his hand on her shoulder wouldn't be disconcerting. It would have been the sort of thing that happened so often that she wouldn't even notice it any more. She couldn't imagine it now, with his palm surely burning a bright red print upon her bare shoulder.

Ally concentrated on breathing, because all of a sudden that was apparently something her body no longer did automatically.

He led her to the front door of the villa and held it open for her while she walked inside. He didn't talk as they crossed the living space and he opened a door into a room that had bifold doors with a balcony beyond, a king-size bed, and a low, wooden-framed couch and chairs arranged around a low coffee table.

The steep slope of the hill meant that although they had walked into the villa at ground level, the ground had dropped away, leaving their room with its own balcony that looked out towards the lake and the mountains beyond. An enormous cantilevered parasol provided shade, and the two sun loungers promised privacy.

She breathed a sigh of relief at finally being out of a situation that had made her so tense she wasn't sure her shoulders were ever going to return to their original position.

'That was—'

'Extremely awkward?' Caleb offered, crossing over to the couch and dropping onto it. He leaned forward, his elbows on his thighs, and watched her closely as she sat in an armchair opposite him. 'I'm sorry. I know I froze—I panicked. Normally I'd just say hello and leave but this is your holiday too and I don't want you to have to if that wasn't what you wanted.'

'I was only going to say it was intense,' she amended, 'and I'm here to help *you* out, remember? We can just carry on as you would if I weren't here if you want.'

'Do you think they bought it?' Caleb asked, looking up and meeting her eye.

Ally considered the question. 'I don't see why they wouldn't. I don't think many people meet their brother's new girlfriend and think that they're faking it. They're not looking for lies so they'll just give us the benefit of the doubt if we stumble. I don't think you have anything to worry about. But are *you* still happy with what we agreed? Because I would hate for you to think that you have to go on with this just because you agreed to it before.'

Caleb shook his head, reaching a hand out towards her, before realising that he hadn't had a plan for what to do with it, and letting it fall back onto his knee. 'No. It's fine. I'm not used to spending much time with them. I prefer to do my own thing, especially when I'm here. I don't think I'd know how to be around you in person for the first time anyway—it was always going to be a bit strange—and now we're faking a relationship. I wish we'd had some more time just us, together, before we did this.'

'I guess,' Ally said thoughtfully. 'We have time now though. Do you want to talk about the family thing?'

Caleb sighed. 'Not really, but I've dragged you here. You should at least know what you're dealing with.'

'You didn't drag me,' she said, putting a hand on his knee, just a small reminder that she was on his side. 'I wanted to come. I jumped at the chance, if you remember.'

He shook his head, and she couldn't quite work out why he was disagreeing with that. She'd got on a plane herself, travelled to a different country, just to hang out with him. He could hardly question that she was here of her own volition.

'It suits us all if I do my own thing. When we're in the same house I try and keep out of their way. But it's not like I spend all my time locked away like a moody teenager. Sure, I work a lot. But I go to the gym, I go running, I go sailing, when I can find the time. But it's only when we're all together

Jonathan thinks that he has to…be a father to me or something. I don't want him feeling like that so it's better that I keep to myself. And now that they're all coupled up, I'm only in the way.'

'What makes you think that they don't want you around?' Ally asked, her brows pinching together. 'They were practically bouncing with excitement when I got here. I think they would have grilled us all afternoon if I'd not made a strategic exit for us.'

'It's not that they don't want me around. It's that they worry about me when I am. I don't like to make them worry so it's easier if I'm not with them so much.'

'Don't all families worry about each other? I admit I'm not exactly the authority on worrying about people the normal amount.'

Caleb gave something that might have passed for a smile if it had reached anywhere close to his eyes.

'Yeah, but my brothers and sisters shouldn't have to act like they're my parents. You know my actual parents left when I was still at school, right? Well, Jonathan ended up doing all the parenting after that, and inheriting a teenager isn't exactly what he had planned for his twenties. And ever since Liv started seeing Adam she seems to think that she also needs to start taking responsibility for me or something like that.'

'None of that is your fault though, Caleb. You didn't have a choice in it any more than they did.'

'I know that. But it didn't stop me seeing what a burden I was to them. How much it cost them to care for me. I don't want to do that to them any more than I have to. To anyone, for that matter.'

'Which is why you're bringing home a fake girlfriend rather than a real one,' Ally said, understanding more about him than he was saying out loud.

'Yeah.'

It turned out, he loved watching Ally think. It was as if he could see right through her skull to the whirring cogs beneath, as each individual thought flitted across her features. So much so that when she spoke, he jumped in surprise.

'I've been thinking,' Ally said, after a few minutes. 'Maybe you'd feel more comfortable about being around your family if we were more comfortable around each other.'

Caleb frowned. 'I'm not uncomfortable around you.'

'No, I mean, if we were more comfortable around each other as a couple. I think I need to get used to it—to us—before we go back out there. And I think it would help you too.'

'Okay, I can see where you're coming from,' he said, thinking her words over. 'But we're treading a fine line between our real friendship, and...the thing that we're faking for our families. So I think we should be very specific about what we mean by "comfortable".'

'Well, I just thought, when you put your arm around my shoulder, it was distracting... Just because it was new. Different. I think we want things like that to feel normal, like it would if we were really together.'

'Okay, I get it, I think. So we, what? Practise hugging? That sounds a little weird.'

'Okay then, not practise. Just...acclimatise to it. Is that better? Just so I don't do something that gives us away. We need to take pictures for my family and they'll be poring over them, looking for any sign that this isn't what I told them it was.'

'So, what was it that made you freeze? When I put my arm around your shoulder? I mean, if I do this now—'

He leaned forward and rested his hands on her hips, used them to pull her closer until her front just brushed against his. She looked up and met his eye, and he tried not to think about how much he liked looking at her from this angle. How affected he was just by her being close to him.

'Or, no, it was more like this,' he said quickly, moving her onto the couch by his side, tucking her under his arm. She linked her arms around his waist and looked up.

'So, how do you feel? Still weird?' he asked.

'Not weird,' she said.

'You might want to think about telling your shoulders that,' he mumbled, stroking a hand down them. She took a deep breath and let her shoulders fall. Tried sinking into the hug rather than fighting it. Caleb's body was warm where it was pressed against her side. He let his arms come around her and rested his head on the top of hers, and some-how she could feel that he was smiling.

'This is nice,' Ally said, her voice muffled in his T-shirt.

He mumbled an agreement. 'I can live with this,' he said back.

She pulled away and slipped her hand into his.

'What's this?' he asked as she pushed him down flat onto the couch and tucked her body into the small space next to his, her head lying on his chest. One hand coming to rest on his thigh.

'Not that different,' he observed once they were settled and his body had relaxed.

'So you're not freaking out any more?'

'No,' he said, a little too quickly. 'It's just a hug. Friends hug.'

'Right. So if we're comfortable with this, then what next?' Ally asked.

'Should we try kissing again?' he replied, with an audible gulp. 'Because unless you're going to keep kissing me like a maiden aunt that might need a little work.'

'Right. We just need to get a few out of the way so that we don't look all awkward.'

'Makes sense, so…' Caleb stroked a finger along her jawline and then cupped his hand around her cheek, turning her face up to him.

'Okay,' Ally said, sounding businesslike in a way that Caleb definitely wasn't feeling. 'This is good. This is fine.'

Caleb was about to lean in, and then stopped, held back for a minute. Because they were alone. In his house. Metres from a king-size bed. He had Ally's body pressed up against him and a thousand thoughts flitting through his mind for how that circumstance could play out. They all started with a kiss like this, and he wasn't sure he could trust himself to go through with this without wanting more. 'Caleb,' Ally breathed. 'Do you think you can at least pretend that you're not repulsed by the thought of this and just get on with it?'

'Oh, my God, would you just—?' He clasped his hands to both sides of Ally's face, turned her mouth up to his and kissed her, sure and hard at first, taking her so much by surprise that she didn't even close her eyes. And then his mouth turned gentle, tender, moving against her lips as if he wanted to explore every curve, parting them gently with his own and then teasing her with his tongue. She groaned and opened to him, her body arching into his as she stretched up to reach him better, one hand coming to the back of his neck, the other to tangle into his hair, which fell in soft waves to his jawline. She was aware that her breasts were crushed against his chest and didn't care in the slightest. If he was going to effortlessly ravish her mouth like this, what was the harm?

'I am absolutely the opposite of repulsed. Okay?' he said breathlessly when he finally pulled away, and it took Ally a moment of stunned silence to remember what he was even talking about.

'Okay,' Ally said, a little dazed, touching her fingertips to her mouth. 'Okay,' she repeated. And then she leaned forward and kissed *him*, this time. More gently, more sweetly than Caleb's kiss.

It was inevitable that Caleb should wrap his arms around her waist and hold her tightly against his body as he explored her mouth with his, all the time trying to remember that this wasn't real. It was fake— or had they decided that it wasn't? He wasn't getting anywhere near enough oxygen to really think about it properly. He pulled away, gasping in a deep breath, and saw his own surprise and confusion reflected in her expression. Ally pulled back just as Caleb's hands brushed over her hips. He left them there as she looked up at him, their eyes locked.

'I think we're okay with that one,' Caleb said, still with a slight tremble in his voice. 'Better than okay. No chance of anyone thinking that we're faking it.'

'We're *really good* at that,' Ally said, a little shakily. 'We probably don't need any more practice.'

'That's a shame,' he said, without thinking.

'Is that your way of telling me you want to kiss me again?'

'No.'

Half of his brain had already closed the shutters and pulled Ally into bed before he remembered they'd agreed that would be a bad idea. So he sat back up and shifted along the couch a little, trying to kid himself that that small amount of space would be enough to get that thought out of his head.

'No, just, that was good. Fine. That was fine. We should probably, you know, go back out with the others…'

'Yeah, yes,' Ally said eventually, shaking her head. 'We should…be around other people. Yes.'

They walked back through the villa, and Caleb gave her a tour. 'This is the bathroom,' he said, his voice clipped as he opened the door from the bedroom into a bathroom with a whirlpool tub and a walk-in shower that he would be turning to ice cold as soon as he had the chance. From there they went through to the open-plan living space with a kitchen in one corner, and low couches around a large, square coffee table. 'That's Jonathan and Rowan's room, Liv and Adam are through there. Dining terrace through the double doors and gym downstairs. I think that's pretty much it,' he said as he opened the double doors to show Ally the dining terrace, which was cooler and shadier than his room at this time of day.

Caleb took a few deep breaths as they walked back out to the pool, his hand still caught in Ally's. He went to force the smile that he usually faked around his family, until he realised that he was already smiling. It had nothing to do with the kiss, he told himself. He was just happy that he was hanging out with his friend, the kissing was entirely incidental to his happiness. Because if it wasn't…that made things so much more complicated, and he needed this to be simple.

He dragged over a couple of loungers to the side of the pool. He pulled his shirt over his head, and when he turned to leave it on the ground next to him he caught the expression on Ally's face. He looked around to make sure that they weren't being watched before he whispered, 'What's wrong?'

But Ally shook her head, her eyes not meeting his.

'Nothing!' she hissed back, before taking a deep breath. 'Nothing,' she repeated more calmly. 'I just didn't know that you, you know, looked like that.'

The corner of his mouth ticked up in an entirely involuntary fashion.

'I told you I go to the gym. A sedentary lifestyle is very bad for your heart.'

She swallowed, dragged her gaze up to his face. 'I'm sorry, I'm just distracted. It's not your fault. I just… I'm distracted.' That quirk of his lip became a full-on smile.

'I think I like having this effect on you,' he said, still smirking.

Ally raised her brows. 'Well, I'm not having you be all smug on me. If I'm distracted then you can be distracted too.' And with that she stood, reached for the hem of her sundress and pulled it over her head.

He audibly gasped at the sight of her: soft stomach, dimpled thighs, breasts barely contained by the deep plunging neckline of her swimsuit. Caleb gulped, pulling on his sunglasses. 'Okay, now I guess things are fair.'

Ally giggled first, and when he looked over she was leaning back on her lounger, soaking up the sun like a kitten who was very pleased with itself.

'Ally! Caleb!' a voice called from behind them. 'We're going to walk into the village, do you want to come?'

Ally looked over at Caleb with her eyebrow raised, but he shook his head.

'Caleb just promised me a swim,' she called back. 'But maybe tomorrow?'

'Sure,' Rowan said, smiling at her. 'We'll come join you in the pool when we get back.'

'You didn't want to go to the village?' Ally asked him when Rowan had gone, because solitude felt as if it was maybe not the best idea after they had discovered that they were mutually speechless at the sight of one another without clothes on and also excellent at kissing.

'I'd really rather not,' Caleb said. 'I think I like your idea better, and we did only just get here.'

'I've got a question,' Ally said, pulling a bottle of sunscreen she'd brought with her out of her bag. 'Why did you come on holiday with them if you dislike spending time with them so much?'

'I didn't,' Caleb complained, lying back with his arm over his face. 'They came on holiday with me.'

'You're going to have to explain the difference,' Ally said, propping up her legs and rubbing sunscreen into her shins.

'I inherited this place from my grandparents after they died a few years ago,' Caleb explained. A glance at him from the corner of her eye revealed his arm still thrown over his face, as if he was worried about catching sight of her.

'Jonathan got the manor in the Cotswolds and Liv got the house in London. Liv sold hers and invested the money in the family business and Liv and Adam's homeless shelter. I wanted to do the same because there's really no point in keeping this place, considering how rarely it gets used, but I wanted to come out here for a week before I handed it over to the estate agent, just to make sure everything was in order. They invited themselves along.'

'So you'd really rather be here alone?' she asked, moving on to cover her arms and her chest with the lotion.

He pulled his arm away and looked at her from the corner of his eye, before pinking in the cheeks and looking away again. 'Not completely alone. I like having you here.'

She smiled, trying not to read too much into that. He liked having her here as a friend. Just as he had kissed her as a friend, and he had stared at her breasts as a friend...

'So tell me more about the family business. You invested in it too? I read about the launch of the fragrance last year. And now branching out into more beauty lines?' Ally said, desperate for a distraction from her own thoughts. Nothing good could come of that line of thinking. She knew herself too well. The minute she found herself getting too involved, the merest hint that he felt the same way and she would push him away.

'It had a cash-flow problem last year,' Caleb explained. 'Jonathan didn't tell me about it until the whole place was about to go under. I could have helped earlier and saved him all that stress, but he didn't even ask. Now he and Liv, and Rowan and Adam, have turned it around. The fragrance was Liv's baby, and that's how she and Adam met. They've got it all under control, apparently.'

'So you're not involved in the running of the business at all?' Ally asked, and didn't miss the way that he flinched at the question.

'They don't want me to be,' he said, his voice carefully flat.

'Why do you think that?' Ally asked carefully, reaching behind her to try and rub sunscreen under the band of her bikini top.

'Because Jonathan wouldn't even involve me when the company was on the brink of collapse. They feel responsible for me, but they don't come to me when they need help. Why would he want me now that he's got it running smoothly?'

'Because it's a family business, you're an investor and have something valuable to add?'

'I don't need to push him on it. If he wanted me on board he would have asked, he didn't and that's fine.'

'Perhaps he takes the fact that you spend as little time as possible with him as a sign that you don't want to be asked,' Ally suggested, but they stopped talking as they heard voices in the house behind them.

'Do you need help with that?' Caleb asked, gesturing at the sunscreen, and she recognised a change of subject when she heard one.

She held out the bottle, telling herself that this was something completely platonic. Friends did this for each other all the time. She didn't want to burn, and Caleb was just looking out for her. She wasn't thinking already about how Caleb's hands were going to feel on her bare skin, and he wouldn't be thinking about it either. They had both been completely honest with one another about what this was. That they were only interested in friendship and anything else was completely fake.

Of course, it had been harder to remember that when they had been kissing, but it was fine. They had done the sensible thing and put a stop to it. Come out here to the pool. It had all just been so that they could properly play their parts. They weren't doing it because they *wanted to*.

She jumped as cold lotion hit her shoulders. Caleb's hands were brisk at first across her skin, as she sat stiff and upright, picking up first one arm and then the other, held out to her side like nothing more than a scarecrow. But when he reached the back of her neck, where her bikini was tied in a knot, he hesitated. He pulled it carefully down, thumbs sweeping under the fabric, sure and certain once he had made the decision to do it. With his hands pressing into her muscles, learning the shape of her shoulders, her back, Ally let out a low sigh of pleasure without realising what she was doing.

She relaxed into his touch, letting him take her weight, only just stopping herself from giving in to her instincts and leaning back into him, letting her body melt against the length of him. When his hands stopped, it took every ounce of her shaky self-control not to beg him to carry on.

She didn't exhale until her back was covered, and she turned and snatched the sun-cream from his hand before this could get any worse. At least once he was done she could turn face-down on the sun lounger and close her eyes. Let the sun warm her back and her thoughts wash over her. She couldn't look at Caleb. She needed a break from the heat between them. This was going to be an exceptionally long week if they carried on like this. If they couldn't get through something as innocent as sitting by the pool.

After a couple of hours of lying in the sunshine doing absolutely nothing, she realised that she couldn't do this all week. Too much time with her own thoughts gave her mind too many opportunities to torture her. She didn't need the drama of developing feelings for Caleb. She'd had all the feelings she needed when she was a teenager, between nearly dying, then the emotional fallout of her parents witnessing it. What she'd dreamt of, those months of constant fear and pain and her parents' red-rimmed eyes, was a simple life. Preferably, with no one making her the centre of their universe, and all their future happiness depending on her survival—something ultimately out of her control.

She knew how much pain she'd caused her parents when she was ill. And she didn't want to have the power to cause anyone else pain like that. Love and pain and grief were all tied up together with the people who loved her, and she didn't want to add to that number.

All she'd seen of love was the fact that it could cause indescribable trauma. Why would she want that for herself, or for anyone else? She'd decided a long time ago that falling in love wasn't for her. She'd separated kissing and sex from feelings and enjoyed one without the other. So why was she freaking out now about something as insignificant as a kiss?

Because it wasn't insignificant—that much was plain to her. And, judging by his reaction, it hadn't been insignificant for Caleb either. But what was she going to do about these inconvenient feelings? Ignoring them seemed like the best place to start. They had both agreed that they were faking this relationship and any kissing that happened was simply a part of that. There was nothing to stress about, she told herself—again. She took a deep breath and let it out slowly, and before she could take another, there was a rustle beside her, and then a loud splash, and droplets of water hit her back. She turned and looked over her shoulder, the sun in her eyes, to see Caleb's wet head emerging from the pool.

So she wasn't the only one feeling overheated. She shrieked as Caleb came right to the edge of the pool and shook his hair like a wet dog, splashing her again. But his silliness drove out the troubling thoughts she'd been fending off and he was once more her friend. The person who had been making her laugh since they'd first started talking in the online game they'd both been playing when they'd met.

He threw an inflatable at her, a boyish grin on his face.

'Come for a swim,' he said, propping his

arm on the side of the pool. Ally looked at him over her sunglasses.

'And why would I want to do that?' she asked dryly.

'Because it's fun,' he said. 'And cool. Come and play.'

She sat up and narrowed her eyes. 'Play what?' she asked suspiciously.

Ally felt her cheeks heat, and crossed to the pool, sitting beside where Caleb was resting by the edge, letting her toes, her feet, then her calves dip in the water.

'What were you planning?' Ally asked. 'Water polo? Synchronised diving?'

Caleb first grinned and then flicked more droplets of water in her face. 'I just want to hang out. Talk. Be normal.'

She smiled, because that was what she'd wanted for this week too—just a chance to hang out with her friend. So she slipped into the water and glided lazily away from the side, drifting on her back.

'I like being your friend better when I don't have to look at your ugly mug,' she said, and he launched himself at her. She squealed, diving under the water and swimming a length of the pool, until she was forced to surface to take a breath, and when she did, there was Caleb, with his arms ready to wrap around her waist and pull her under, amidst a shout of protest and a rush of bubbles.

'Ugly mug,' he scoffed as they surfaced again, his arms still round her waist.

It's not real. None of this is real, she told herself, concentrating on the fact that she was here to finally hang out in person with her best friend rather than the fact that the feel of his hands on her waist was making her forget that the water was cold. She withdrew herself from his arms and they swam a few lazy lengths side by side before Caleb got out and pulled a couple of lilos into the pool and she clambered onto one of them, then reached out a hand for the cocktail that Caleb had just poured her.

Then he was floating on an inflatable next to her, and she pulled down her white plastic-rimmed sunglasses and shut her eyes, letting the hand not holding her drink trail through the water. She could sense Caleb beside her, and smiled to herself, feeling supremely contented with her life in that moment. She had been overreacting about those kisses. This was totally fine. More than fine. This was an Italian villa and hot sunshine and a cold drink. It was an escape from the pressure her parents unwittingly heaped on her. She would send them photos of her and her gorgeous boyfriend in his dreamy Italian villa and they couldn't possibly set her up on any more doomed singles cruises. She smiled to herself. She would not let her overactive brain ruin this for her.

'Just think, I could have been at singles line dancing right about now if I hadn't let you talk me into this.'

'Not too late to change your mind. I'm sure we can meet the ship in port somewhere.'

She half-heartedly flicked a few spots of water at him. 'Don't even joke about it,' she scolded him. 'My parents are still not convinced you're good enough for their only daughter. They might book me on again for next year just in case.'

'Well, we'll just have to convince them otherwise, won't we?' he said as his family walked around the corner of the villa and onto the terrace. She saw indecision cross his face, but then he pulled up his sunglasses and shouted across to his sister. 'Hey! Liv! Come take a photo of me and Ally!' She heard his sister groan, but Liv dragged herself away from the group and picked up Caleb's phone from the table.

'Fine, but don't do anything gross,' she said as Caleb pulled Ally's inflatable closer to his own. 'Smile, then,' Liv prompted, and Ally suddenly found herself grinning, not sure whether she looked as if she was faking it or not. She was happy. Having fun. All they needed were a few photos that showed her parents that. But Caleb seemed to have something more complicated in mind and was trying to pull her lilo even closer, reaching an arm to go around her shoulders, leaning in as if he was about to kiss her. She reached a hand to his chest, steadying him before he capsized them both, but he obviously misinterpreted her intentions, and leaned in further. At which point his lilo flipped over. He reached out and grabbed Ally in a misguided attempt to save himself, only to drag her down with him. She was laughing as she hit the water, one hand held high to try and save her drink, until she realised that it was already full of pool water.

'I'm so sorry,' he gasped as he broke the surface of the water. 'Are you okay?'

'That was great, Cal, really slick.' Liv cackled as she followed the others back inside, and Ally towed both lilos to the side of the pool.

'Great job,' Ally told him, laughing, pushing hair first out of her face, and then his, pushing a lock from the corner of his eye. 'My parents are definitely going to love you now that you've half drowned their only daughter.'

She pushed herself out of the pool and accepted the towel that Caleb handed her, squeezing water out of her hair and wishing she could do the same with the moulded cups of her bikini top without looking completely indecent.

Caleb came over and scrubbed at her hair with his towel, and she laughed as she looked up at him.

'I'm sorry,' he said earnestly, still dabbing at the water dripping from her hair onto her shoulders. 'Are you sure you're okay?'

'I'm fine,' she reassured him, sliding her own towel under the strap of her bikini. Caleb's fingers followed the path of her towel, and she looked up at him in surprise. When he reached the edge of her bikini, she held her breath, wondering whether he would venture under the fabric. When she looked up, his desire was written over every feature. His pupils blown wide, his bottom lip caught between his teeth.

There was nothing false about that look. They didn't have an audience. It was just her and Caleb out here. That expression was entirely for her. He was looking at her as if she was the only thing in the universe worth paying attention to. As if he *needed* her. And she couldn't stand it.

'I'm going to go in and dry off,' she said abruptly, wrapping the towel around herself, covering her bikini, the cooling water dripping down her back making her shiver.

For a moment she worried that he was going to follow her inside, and wasn't sure if she was more relieved or disappointed when she was left trying to tease apart the knotted straps of her bikini alone.

CHAPTER THREE

ALLY WAS FREAKING OUT, and he knew that it was his fault. He'd got carried away, hadn't just stepped over a line but thoroughly trampled it, making a mess in the process. What had he been thinking, touching her like that? He had scared her off. Put too much pressure on her, and she had run. He wouldn't be surprised if she came out here with her bags packed and a ticket for the next flight back to London.

He would never forgive himself if he had irreparably harmed their friendship. True, Ally had been the first to fake their relationship, but he was the one who had invited her here. Who had pulled her into his body to practise being close to one another. But that was all it had been. He might have thought that there was something more in it, something beyond the clear parameters that they'd spelled out for one another, but Ally obviously hadn't. He'd gone too far, and now they were going to be awkward and weird with each other. He'd needed too much from her, and that had pushed her away. Every time, he did this. And if he tried to fix things he only managed to make things a hundred times worse, like, for example, trying to kiss her and accidentally capsizing her in the deep end of the pool.

He collapsed on the sun lounger and reached for his phone to see if Liv had taken any pictures that might convince Ally's family that they didn't need to keep meddling with her love life. At least if they had done that she would have got something out of this trip and this friendship he was pretty sure he'd just ruined. He groaned as he swiped through. He looked as if he were actively trying to drown her. Ally looked like she was trying to get as far away from him as possible. His brilliant idea had not been a success.

'That was smoothly done, little brother.'

Liv appeared on the terrace with a couple of beers in hand. He thought about retreating back to his room, but Ally had made clear that she needed space and he wasn't going to go barging in there. He covered his face with his hand, because of course his moment of tragic embarrassment had happened in front of his whole family so that his humiliation was complete. And now he was trapped out here with his sister, who he knew would be merciless about it.

'Liv, be nice,' Rowan scolded her, coming onto the terrace just in time to save him. 'She's lovely, Caleb,' she added. 'We're really happy for you. I'm certain that's what Liv was trying to say.'

Liv snorted beside her, and not even his sweet-as-pie sister-in-law—usually his favourite family member—was going to convince him he wasn't being openly mocked.

'Yeah, well, I think so too,' he said, which wasn't going to count for anything if she was packing her bags even as he spoke. All she'd wanted—perfectly reasonably—was for him to get her out of the hellish-sounding cruise that her parents had booked and he'd spoiled that all because the sight of a water droplet trickling down her skin had been too much for him to resist.

She hadn't asked for emotional complications. This was exactly why he avoided situations like this. The real ones, that was—the fake boyfriend thing didn't actually occur that often. The real boyfriend thing? He'd tried it a few times, but…well.

And that was before he considered who it was he was talking about. This was Ally, who was all but allergic to feelings. He'd been joking about that doctor that her parents had set her up with—but only just. Because he'd got most of the story at the time, and it had sounded an awful lot like as soon as the guy had shown any interest in her, she'd extracted herself from the situation without a backward glance. If she'd thought about the guy since, he couldn't be sure— but she'd never mentioned him again.

He didn't have the full story about her teenage years, or about the difficult relationship with her parents. She'd tell him if she wanted him to know. All he knew was that she bolted at the first sight of complicated emotions—and that his parents had laid the groundwork with what an emotional burden he could be. They'd left the country rather than stick around for his teenage years. The job of seeing him through adolescence had fallen to Jonathan—in school holidays at least—and every line and mark of strain on his older brother's face over the past ten years had shown him what a burden that had been.

He'd thought that doing his own thing and staying out of his family's way was what he should do. But apparently he couldn't even get that right—why else would they have sat him down and asked him whether it was healthy to be spending so much time working, or on his computer? The fact that he'd run his own hugely successful business trading in cryptocurrency since he'd left university hadn't been enough to convince them that he didn't need—or want—their concern. Nor the fact that a huge chunk of that time recently had been spent hanging out with Ally online.

Here he was, with a fake girlfriend, to convince them that he wasn't a kid any more. He wasn't their burden, their responsibility. He wasn't anyone's problem, and that was the way he wanted it to stay. He hated seeing how much loving him had cost the people in his life. Hated the way it hurt when it got too much and they left him. So he knew what he had to do now.

He had to make sure that Ally knew he didn't want a real relationship. If he wanted Ally to stick around, he had to make this simple for her, make her believe that he was no more affected by their kiss than she was. If he let on that he wanted more she would be shutting him out faster than any of the dating-app guys that she'd hooked up with and then left without a backward glance. And he wasn't going to convince her everything was okay by refusing to be in the house with her. He gathered up his things and headed into the villa, thinking that she was probably out of the shower by now.

He knocked quietly at the door—keeping things cool didn't mean walking-in privileges. She was dressed, thank God. Though the whole indifference thing would be easier if she hadn't just pulled on another sundress that wrapped in a deep V across lush breasts and skimmed and flared from generous hips. If he closed his eyes, he could still feel the shape of her in his palms. He flexed his fingers, trying to force the feel-

ing from his muscles. He could just forget…
he could act as if he didn't feel anything
for her.

'What? Is this not okay?' she asked, looking straight down her cleavage, her hands
running over the front of her dress.

'No, it's great,' he said, clearing his throat.

'Then why are you looking at me like
that?'

He knew the fact that he was feeling absolutely stunned would scare her off, he knew
he had to keep his feelings out of this.

'You look great,' he said again.

Ally looked up and her gaze snagged with
his, and he saw her expression heat.

'You're going to have to stop looking at me
like that,' she said, half warning, half threat.

Could she see how desperate he was?
How far his feelings were getting away from
him? How hard he was fighting to keep them
under control and how badly he was failing?
Desperation was just the sort of feeling that
sent Ally running. He had to show her he
was in control of this. He had to *be* in control of this.

'I'm sorry,' he said, pulling his eyes away and trying to make the words sound casual.

'A walk, then?' she suggested, and he nodded. The afternoon had cooled a little and he could keep her out of the sun if they stuck to the shade of the olive and lemon groves. The vineyards he'd save for an early morning, when the sun was still low. They could walk the rows of vines, check the fruit, pretend they were the only people on the planet.

He shook his head. That was dangerously close to romantic.

Dangerously close to the sort of sentiment that would have Ally freezing him out of her life, even as a friend, and he couldn't risk that when he had only just met her for real.

'I'll show you around the grounds,' he said, pulling on trainers and crossing to the doors out onto the terrace. They waved at the others as they passed the pool, Caleb shouting that they were going for a walk, his tone making clear that he wasn't extending them an invitation.

'It's so beautiful here,' Ally said as they walked among the olive trees, Caleb sticking to the shade and watching Ally's shoulders for signs of turning pink. He should probably ask if she needed more sunscreen, but they both knew exactly where that would lead, and he didn't trust himself to go there.

'You're really selling this place?' Ally asked, turning to look at him. He leant back against the trunk of a tree, letting it take his weight as he watched Ally wander through the trees. 'Won't you miss it?'

'We hardly use it. And even if we did, it wouldn't be right. Liv and Adam have started a new foundation to support people experiencing homelessness. We all decided that we wanted to keep the house in the Cotswolds. It's been in the family for the longest, Rowan and Jonathan just got married there, and Adam and Liv will have their wedding there in the autumn. I have a little place in London and Liv and Adam have a garden flat near the office. Rowan and Jonathan live in the Cotswolds and commute. I can't see how we can justify keeping this place too when there are people out there without even somewhere safe to sleep.'

'I guess that's true,' Ally said, and dropped to sit cross-legged in the shade of the tree opposite. 'So you helped finance the family business and you're selling this place for Liv's foundation. Wouldn't it be cheaper and easier to just tell your family that you care about them?'

He'd pushed off from the tree and taken half a step towards her before he realised what he was doing. 'I don't know what you're talking about,' he snapped before he could stop himself. 'That's got nothing to do with it. I'm just trying to do the right thing. At this point my investments are making money faster than I can give it away. Why wouldn't I use it to help my family?'

'Of course you want to help your family,' Ally said, looking at him thoughtfully from her seat beneath the tree. 'And if you were capable of having a conversation with them as well as throwing money at the situation, I wouldn't be asking the question.'

He bristled, crossing his arms over his chest. 'I'm perfectly capable of having a conversation with them. I don't know why you'd think I'm not.'

She laughed, but it sounded a little brittle,

more than a little forced. 'Um, maybe because all the available evidence proves me right. You've not voluntarily spent a minute with them since we got here. You told me yourself you'd rather they hadn't come.'

'Ally, you've been here for less than a day. What can you possibly know about it?' he said, knowing that it wasn't true. That she knew him better than he was comfortable with. If she hadn't been here in person—if they'd been able to have this conversation safely, with a screen between them—then he wouldn't be taking it like this. He would have thought about what she was saying. Thought about his answer. Replied in a reasoned and sensible fashion. But he couldn't do that when she was here, so very much in the flesh, confusing everything he thought he knew about his feelings for her.

'Don't do that,' Ally snapped in warning. 'Don't pretend our friendship started when you picked me up from the airport. I know you know better than that.'

He stared at her for a moment, wondering whether to quit or double down. But he couldn't do that. He couldn't just throw away their friendship. He imagined what his life would look like without her in it. Without someone to share his day with, even through a screen. He couldn't bear it.

'Ally, I'm sorry,' he said. 'You know I don't think that. You know how important you were to me long before we got here.'

Her expression softened, and he took another few steps and dropped to sit beside her.

'Then stop acting like I don't know you,' she chided, knocking his shoulder with hers. Taking a deep breath and then letting her head come down to rest on his shoulder. 'I don't like it when you pretend you're someone other than the Caleb that I know I know.'

'I know that you know me. But I don't see how you can know about my relationship with my family. I've barely spoken to you about them,' he explained.

'And you think that doesn't say anything about how you feel about them? I've seen you all together and how much they obviously care about you, and then I see you lying to them about us, and it makes me wonder why you don't just talk to them.'

'Like you do with your parents?' he shot

back, keeping his face as innocent as he could, knowing that his deflection was as good as starting a fight.

'We weren't talking about me,' Ally pointed out, her voice terse.

Which meant that he was on the right track. That he could lead this discussion away from his own failings. 'Well, maybe we should have been. You've never given me the full story on why we're lying to them anyway,' he said.

'If I'm honest with you, will you return the favour?' Ally asked, and he hesitated. Because that would be fair, wouldn't it? But opening up to Ally, being vulnerable with her, that wasn't going to do anything but burden her with things that she couldn't fix. Talking to her wasn't going to change the fact that responsibility for looking after him had been dumped on Jonathan without him asking for it. He couldn't undo the years that Jonathan had lost worrying about him, trying to keep the business afloat without his help because he didn't want Caleb drawn into the mess. And if he couldn't stop Jonathan fretting, he could at least stop anyone else feeling as though they had to worry about him too.

'I don't really understand why you're so keen to talk about my family,' he said carefully. 'But, sure. Show me yours and I'll show you mine.'

Ally sighed, leaned back and closed her eyes. She wanted to distance herself from him—and, fine. He could understand that. He should have expected that. 'Well, you know I was sick as a kid?' she asked, and he murmured a yes. Because she'd mentioned it, in passing, before. Glancing words, never enough detail for him to build a real picture of what she had gone through.

'You've mentioned it, but not the details,' he prompted her.

'Well. It's not fun to talk about,' she said, eyes still closed, an arm thrown over them now. 'It was bad. I had leukaemia and they were pretty certain that I wasn't going to make it. I was close, too close, to not making it. By the time I got the bone marrow transplant that I needed, no one actually thought that I could come back from how sick I was. My parents were already grieving for me, I think, even before I was gone.'

'I'm sorry,' he said, reaching for her hand and giving it a squeeze. He couldn't help it. She wanted space, and that was fine, but he didn't want her to think that she was alone. She opened her eyes, turned her head towards him and smiled before pulling her hand back.

'Don't be sorry,' she said with a smile he was sure she'd performed hundreds of times. 'I'm fine now. I made it! I hardly ever think of it—it isn't really what this is about.'

'Can you explain what it is, then? Because not to be...you know, all self-involved, but... How do I come into this?'

She laughed, and he wondered again how he'd been her friend for so long without hearing that sound. He valued what their friendship had been before they had met in person. It hadn't been any less real just because it had happened online. But now that he'd done this, he wasn't sure that he'd be able to go back to being satisfied with emojis. Without hearing her laugh again.

'What's that look for?' Ally asked, suddenly looking suspicious, narrowing her eyes at him.

'Nothing bad. Just enjoying you being here,' he admitted.

There was no way she could cover her blush on that skin, sunshine glow or not.

'Aren't you supposed to be interrogating me about my tragic childhood?' she reminded him.

Caleb nodded lazily. 'I can if you want, but the option to just…offer up information is there too, you know. If you wanted this to be more like a regular conversation. I want to listen.'

'Okay, fine.' Ally gave way with a sigh. 'Where were we? I nearly died, my mum and dad were devoted to me. Gave up their own lives to be with me. Spent every day in the hospital with me. I was the centre of their universe, making memories. You get the picture. And every time they looked at me like I had sunbeams shining from every orifice, I knew that they were thinking about when I wouldn't be there any more. It wasn't about me, not really. It was about shoring themselves up for when I was dead.'

'That sounds…impossibly hard,' Caleb said, trying to imagine it.

'It sounds so ungrateful,' Ally said, shaking her head. 'I should just be glad that I survived it. That they survived it. And, honestly, I am. But every time someone looks at me like that, like I'm the centre of their world and their whole lifetime of happiness depends on me just existing—I can't. And they're desperate for me to fall in love and have children of my own. To have all the things that they thought that I would have lost by dying too young. But why would I want that? Why would I want anyone else to love me when I see what loving me did to my parents? Why would I want to love someone when I've seen how much it can hurt? It's too much pressure and it's too much pain. No, thank you. I think I like things how they are.'

'I'm sorry, Ally. That sounds like it would be a lot for anyone to bear.'

'I know that it's just because they love me! And I should be grateful for that! And they just want what's best for me! But honestly the crushing pressure of having to be happy as well as alive because they're waiting, watching for me to fulfil all this potential that I was never even meant to have. I genuinely don't know what to do with all this *hope* that they have invested in me. I just want to be loved a normal amount,' she said finally.

He nodded, thinking through her words. 'I think I can understand that.'

'But isn't that what you've got with your family?'

'Loving me a normal amount? No. I don't think I have. If we were a normal family they'd barely have to think of me. I'd just be the annoying little brother who usually showed up late to stuff. But Jonathan ended up having to parent me and that pretty much ruined his twenties, and I can't undo that.'

'Is that how he sees it? Have you asked him?'

'I don't need to; I was there. I saw it all first-hand. But we were talking about you. I'm sorry that your parents don't listen to you. That they don't respect your choices.'

'Your turn,' Ally said, shaking her head as if she could shake her thoughts away. 'Why are we faking this for *your* family? Why not just date someone for real?'

He sighed into his forearm. 'Because "I don't want to" is good enough for you but not for me?'

She frowned and pulled his arm away, fixing him with a look that was too hard to look away from. 'That's not all I said and you know it.'

'Okay, fine. I don't like to date,' he said. 'It's hard to see how you can love someone without it turning into a situation where you end up causing them more hassle than it's worth.'

He had to look away from the understanding expression on Ally's face. So both of them were going to resist this pull between them. Well, good. That was a good thing, because if this was dependent on him holding himself back, he wasn't sure that it was going to work.

'So you have an end date to save you from the disaster that falling for me would be,' Caleb said, trying to laugh.

'You're not a burden,' Ally said, looking deadly seriously at him. 'Your siblings don't just worry about you. They love you,' Ally added, as if that were in question. 'They want you to be in their lives.'

'Of course they do,' Caleb said, shaking his head. 'I know that. The problem is that I don't *want* them to. Not when I know what it costs. I hate that loving me means that I can hurt people. I don't want to do that to anyone else. I know that you understand this, Ally, so I don't know why you're trying to convince me to change.'

She half smiled, one corner of her mouth turning up. 'So does that mean we're not talking about our feelings any more?'

'I think you should be honest with me about how you felt before you walked away from me earlier, after getting out of the pool. If we're not honest with each other, things could get confusing. You need to tell me if I overstepped, or... I don't know. I just think we should talk about it.'

Ally pushed the heels of her hands into her eyes. She didn't have to ask what he was talking about.

'I think... I don't know. It was more confusing than I was expecting, having you touch me like that. I thought that we would be able to compartmentalise what was fake and what was real, but it wasn't that easy. I mean, a friend who you kiss is more than a friend, right? And you were looking at me like you wanted me and... It's hard that one part of that is the most real thing I have in my life, and the other is completely fake. It's hard to learn two ways to be around each other and remember to do the right one at the right time, but we'll get there. I know we will.'

He sat with her words. He could see her thinking, still turning them over and trying to find a solution for them. 'I understand,' he said carefully. 'And I feel the same way, but I don't think that just because it's difficult we have to call the whole thing off. It's okay for us to admit that it's hard, and to keep trying. We can practise a little at a time. Take things slow.'

She looked up at him. 'So you're saying that I'm freaking out over nothing and that if we just talk about our feelings everything would be much simpler? I don't know, that sounds too easy.'

Caleb laughed. 'It's got to be worth a try. And I didn't say that you freaked out over nothing. Just that maybe if we talked more, there would be no need to freak out in the first place.'

'And we both know how we feel about relationships,' Ally added. 'So we both know there's no danger of either of us wanting more than the other does, even if the lines get blurred at times.'

'Right,' Caleb tried, reaching for Ally's hand, turning it over and pretending to inspect the palm. He ran the pad of a finger across the creases before lacing their fingers together. 'So we keep practising holding hands until it feels completely natural. And neither of us is going to think that it's a big deal, or if we do then we'll talk about it and it won't be a problem. And if we touch in a more than friendly way, even when no one's around, it's just because it's sometimes hard to keep things straight. It doesn't have to mean anything. Once this week is over we'll just go back to normal and everything will be fine.'

'Exactly,' Ally said, looking down at their joined hands. 'And neither of us is going to freak out about the way that I looked at you earlier, because it didn't mean anything and it's not going to lead anywhere we don't want it to.'

'This week we're hanging out and having fun. Next week we go back to avoiding human company.'

Ally pressed a kiss to his knuckles. 'And all this time I've been telling my mother the perfect man doesn't exist.'

She stood and pulled him up. The sun was lower than when they'd entered the grove, the shadows a lot longer. When they reached the villa, the furniture around the pool had been tidied into neat clusters. Empty glasses and bottles cleared away.

The delicious smells of garlic, butter and lemon were emerging from the kitchen, where Adam and Liv seemed to be squabbling over a frying pan on the stove. Ally couldn't help but smile at their easy intimacy. She might not want it for herself, but that didn't mean she didn't recognise real love when it was right in her face. And she saw what she was sure Caleb didn't or wouldn't—that they were all delighted that Caleb was there with them. She had no interest in changing Caleb's mind about romantic relationships—but she wasn't sure that she would be able to leave this alone. She couldn't leave him believing that his family would be happier without him in their lives. She knew that she wouldn't be happier without him. As a friend. It was important to keep reminding herself of that.

She'd assumed that Caleb would be dragging her off to their room, but he pulled up a seat at the dinner table and poured himself a glass of wine. Perhaps he made an exception when food was involved.

Or perhaps he was thinking over what she'd said and was making an effort.

Dinner passed without incident, though without a lot of conversation from Caleb, and it was only as Liv produced some local limoncello, in a bottle without a label, that Ally remembered when this meal was over they would be sharing a room—perhaps they should have talked about sleeping arrangements before they'd started on the wine. She glanced across the table at Caleb, wondering if he was thinking about it too. Probably not, because they were just friends sharing a bed, nothing more dramatic than that. She really didn't need to blow this out of proportion.

She passed on the second round of limoncello though, because lowering her inhibitions didn't seem like the best idea. The combination of pasta, red wine and limoncello was making her eyelids heavy, but it wasn't until Caleb's hand on her shoulder made her jolt that she realised that she'd been drifting off even while she was still sitting up.

'You look shattered,' he said gently, standing behind her with his hands settled comfortably on her shoulders. 'Ready for bed?'

She didn't have enough brainwaves still awake and functioning to form words. Instead she let out a tired little sigh. When she looked up at Caleb, his face was warm and affectionate. He reached a hand down to help her up. 'Come on, sleepy head.' He towed her out of her chair with a less than flattering little grunt. Everyone called goodnight as he steered her down the hallway with his hands on her hips and then reached past her to open the bedroom door.

'Why didn't you tell me you were so tired?' he asked, kicking the door closed behind them and leading her over to the bed. He'd turned the air con up earlier, and somehow it was now arctic in here. Ally shivered and goosebumps prickled on her arms.

He pushed her into the bathroom, along

with the oversized T-shirt she slept in, grabbed hastily from her bag, and shut the door.

They were just friends, Caleb reminded himself. Friends who were in a fake relationship that had required that they practise kissing earlier, meaning that now he couldn't pretend he didn't know how good it felt to have his hands, his mouth on her.

He smiled indulgently as the door to the bathroom opened and Ally leaned against the frame. Her T-shirt stretched over generous breasts, skimmed her tummy, and ended above soft dimpled thighs. She was utterly delicious. Or, at least, that was what he would have been thinking if he really had been her boyfriend, rather than just a friend that she'd decided to fake feelings for.

But as he met her eyes and she leaned against the doorframe, he realised that she was already half asleep. He turned back the sheets on the bed and grabbed a blanket from the wardrobe.

'You get in the bed,' he told her as she crossed her arms over her chest and rubbed her upper arms. 'Sorry about the air con.

I've turned it down so it'll warm up in here soon. I'll sleep on the couch.'

After he was done in the bathroom, he came back into the bedroom and found Ally still awake despite her exhaustion. The shape of her body was visible through the sheet and thin blanket, lying on her side, hugging her knees.

'I'm sorry it's so cold,' he said again earnestly, brushing a hand over her cheek before he could stop himself. 'You're freezing!' he announced, and felt ridiculous—because of course she already knew that.

'Get in,' she said, wrapping her arms tighter around herself. 'Please?' she mumbled, shivering. 'Just until I warm up?'

He hesitated, but it really was freezing in here, and he couldn't leave her literally shivering and asking for his help. So he grabbed more blankets from the wardrobe, climbed in the other side of the bed and wrapped his arms around her waist, pulling her close.

His arms learned the shape of her as he tucked her head under his chin and inhaled the scent of her—chlorine and sunscreen and limoncello. It was a friendly gesture to keep her warm, he repeated to himself as her shivering stopped and skin smoothed under his hands. 'Better?' he asked, and heard a gentle snore as his answer.

Just a friend. Just a friend, he told himself as he started to pull himself away. He had told her that he would sleep on the couch, and he wasn't going to share a bed with her under false pretences.

He tried to ease himself away, to give them both a little space. He wasn't sure that Ally had meant for them to sleep like this. She'd just temporarily needed him for his body heat and the last thing he wanted to do was take advantage. He reached behind him to turn off the lamp. Probably for the best, he thought, letting out a long breath that ruffled the hairs on the top of her head. But as he went to get out of bed, Ally just snuggled back harder, her softly rounded bottom rubbing against him in a way that was decidedly more than friendly and was not at all going to help him sleep.

'Ally?' he whispered, in case she'd woken and he'd just not realised. But she didn't reply, just wrapped her arms more tightly around his and made any chance of moving impossible. He took a deep breath and willed sleep to come, or for Ally to wake up, or for his erection to subside. One way or another, this was going to be a long night.

CHAPTER FOUR

ALLY WAS WARM. Her memory returned in bits and pieces. She was warm because she was in Italy, she was in Italy because of Caleb. And the hardness pressing against her back was because... Oh. She glanced down and saw her arms wrapped tightly around his, caging his forearms across her stomach. She released them suddenly, looking at her hands as if they didn't belong to her. Disloyal things. Well, she hadn't asked them to pull Caleb close and hold him there. They'd taken the initiative on that. This was so mortifying. Except...from what she could feel behind her, Caleb didn't seem to be complaining. That didn't mean anything. It was just a physiological thing. When Caleb woke up he was going to be as embarrassed about this as she was.

'Mmm...' She heard gentle waking sounds

from behind her and held her breath wondering how she could extract herself in the seconds, probably, before Caleb woke up and realised what they'd done in the night. How she'd tucked herself into him and pressed back against his body. Wrapped her arms around his so he couldn't get away even if he'd wanted to. She listened to his breathing change, and then felt the tension through his body as he came to wakefulness and realised how they were lying.

'Morning?' she whispered into the dark, closing her eyes with embarrassment even though she couldn't see him.

'Hey, good morning. Oh…um…sorry,' Caleb offered from somewhere behind her, his arms suddenly springing from around her waist. 'God, sorry, Ally. I'll…' She turned over so that she could see him, putting the space they needed between them to be able to hold a conversation without dying from embarrassment. 'I'm sorry,' Caleb said again, and Ally lifted a hand to his cheek.

'Hey, it's all right. Nothing to apologise for,' she said, trying to add some lightness to her voice. 'It's just morning, and I'd made myself pretty comfortable and…now I'm rambling.'

Caleb laughed, a quiet little huff of air that she wouldn't have been able to hear if she'd not been sharing a pillow with him. She pulled her hand away from his face, tucking it safely under her cheek where it couldn't be tempted to stray and make trouble.

'You were cold,' he explained. 'Do you remember? Because of the air con. And I tried to move once you were asleep, but—'

'I aggressively spooned you? I'm sorry, I should have warned you that I do that sometimes. I would have, but I didn't expect to wipe out like that.'

'Let's just forget about it,' Caleb suggested. And sure, yes, perhaps it could just be as easy as that. 'What do you want to do today?' he asked, and Ally took that to mean that simply being half naked in bed together all day wasn't one of the options on offer.

'Do you really have a speedboat?' she asked hopefully.

'I really have a speedboat,' he confirmed.

'Want to show it to me?' Ally asked, in a way that she hoped wasn't too suggestive.

'I suppose it's too late now to try and

protect my modesty,' Caleb admitted with a groan. 'Sure, I'll show you my speedboat. Want to pack a picnic? Make a day of it?'

She narrowed her eyes at him. 'So that you don't have to spend time with your siblings?'

He tapped the end of her nose with his fingertip. 'Because once you're out in the middle of that lake you aren't ever going to want to come back. I'm not going to let you starve.'

'Fine,' Ally agreed.

'Fine.'

'Good.'

'Good.'

Ally paused. 'You haven't got up.'

'Nor have you,' Caleb replied.

No, she hadn't, because she was in bed with a nice guy. But a speedboat was a speedboat.

'You, um. You should go first,' Caleb said, his cheeks turning pink. 'While I shut my eyes and count slowly to ten.'

'Right. Right!' Ally said, her voice a high-pitched squeal. She edged away from him across the bed, the sheet clutched to her even though she was perfectly well covered by her T-shirt. 'I'll…um…just…go.'

She jumped from the bed, ripping the Band-Aid off, knowing that letting herself linger wasn't going to lead to sensible decision-making.

Caleb grazed through the fridge, looking for delicacies to add to the cooler he was packing to take out on the boat with them. It was moments like this that reminded him there were vast swathes of the friendship landscape that were missing. He had spent more hours than he could count talking to Ally, knew her taste, how she liked to be kissed, the shape of her hips. But he didn't know if she liked olives. Whether he should pack ice-cold lemonade or beer or prosecco.

He rubbed at the back of his neck as he stared into the fridge, wondering what it meant that he could know her so well in some ways, and not at all in others. In the end, he packed the cool box indiscriminately. He might not know what she liked, but there was one sure way to find out. That was what this week could be—getting to know one another. And in the daytime, that could mean learning what she liked in a picnic. At night? He shivered. He couldn't even let himself think about what he might learn in the six nights that they had left together.

'How long have you been staring into the fridge? You've got goosebumps,' Ally said, appearing behind him.

Better that she thought they were a result of the cold, rather than the direction his thoughts had just taken. 'Ooh, olives,' she said, reaching past him to snag a jar from the top shelf. 'Yum. You weren't leaving these behind, were you?' she asked and added them to the cooler.

It could be as easy as that, then. The more time they spent together, the more this friendship would feel like something solid and real. Perhaps by the end of the week it would feel just…normal to be around her. This weirdly expectant feeling in his gut would disappear and being around her would feel less like something he should be afraid of.

The worst part was, he couldn't talk about it to the one person every instinct he had desperately wanted to talk to. Her.

'Are you sure you're okay?' Ally asked,

and he realised that he hadn't answered her question.

'I'm fine,' he said, plastering on a smile to hide his confusion. 'Just thinking if there's anything else we need. Have you got sunscreen? A hat?'

'Yes, Mother.' She slapped a hat on top of her strawberry-blonde waves, and he realised he hadn't properly looked at her since she'd walked into the kitchen. She was wearing a navy-and-white-striped vest top, which revealed the red halter strap of her bathing suit beneath. And shorts. Short shorts. Cut-off denims that revealed an expanse of soft, pale, dimpled thigh that made him want to drop to his knees and worship them.

He drew his gaze away with what little self-control he had left and pulled his sunglasses down from the top of his head for good measure. Deep breaths. Seriously deep breaths.

He was aware of the questioning look that Ally was sending in his direction, and that the fact that the sight of her thighs made it all but impossible to breathe meant that...

'What can I carry?' Ally asked, but he picked up the cooler in one hand and the bag of towels in the other. Ally rolled her eyes at him.

'I'm not going to argue about the cooler because I've seen your muscles and you are absolutely the best person for the job. But I can carry a bag of towels. Hand them over.'

He passed her the bag with a grudging expression. 'I'm trying to be a good boyfriend.'

That startled a laugh out of her, and she pressed a quick kiss to his cheek.

'You are being an excellent boyfriend. Stop worrying.'

Caleb kept sneaking looks at her as they walked across the terrace, and then down the steps to the dock where the boat was moored.

Ally stopped in her tracks. 'You know, a less generous woman might worry that you were over-compensating for something,' she said when the boat came into view.

He bumped her shoulder with his.

'Hey, I've got nothing to prove.'

She smirked. 'Yes, well. I think I found that out for myself this morning.'

He felt heat rising in his cheeks at the memories that brought back and couldn't quite meet her eye.

'But this is pretty fancy,' Ally said as Caleb climbed aboard and then reached out a hand to steady her as she stepped over the gunwale and onto the deck.

Caleb shrugged. 'It's a toy and I can barely justify it even to myself. I bought it when my grandparents were still alive, but I've hardly been here the last couple of years so it doesn't get used much.'

'Cal, come on. You're allowed to do nice things for yourself. And if your nice thing is a speedboat to impress all the girls, then all the better for me.'

'Girl,' he corrected, because that seemed like an important distinction to make. 'I've not brought anyone else here.'

This time it was Ally's turn to blush. No, it was probably just the sun.

'Sunscreen,' he said, holding out a hand.

'You've not going to give me a tour before you ask to feel me up?'

He shook his head, laughing. 'I didn't know that talking about our feelings was going to be quite so direct. I'm not trying to feel you up, as you so elegantly put it. Your nose is pink already and I don't want your shoulders going the same way.'

'You know, you're very bossy when you're taking care of me,' she accused, passing him the sunscreen from her bag and turning her back, sweeping her mass of hair over one shoulder.

'Be quiet and move your straps,' he told her, pulling her closer. She might not be able to see him, but she could hear the smile in his voice. Ally rolled her eyes as she pulled the straps of her vest off her shoulders. He was mercifully quick, leaving her half wishing that he'd taken better advantage of the situation. And then his hands were off her skin and she shouldn't be as affected by that as she truly was.

She'd imagined that maybe his hands would linger. That maybe he'd be looking for excuses to touch her because that was what she wanted, deep down, even if she couldn't tell him that. It was simpler if he just gave it to her without her having to admit what she wanted. Because telling him that would mean having to work out for herself first what she really wanted, and she wasn't sure she could look at herself in the mirror and admit to herself that she wanted his hands on her. Wanted him as her best friend, and—yes, if he had been anyone else, perhaps she would have given him an access-all-areas pass to her body. But she couldn't do that with him. He was too precious to her to risk losing. To risk needing to push him away because she'd started to care too much.

Admitting to herself that she cared at all scared her. Acknowledging that there was a chance that she could want more from him would be too much. Her best friend. What would it be like if he were her lover too? She didn't doubt that it would be good. But she also didn't doubt how much she would get hurt if it all fell apart. The sex wouldn't be a problem. But the wanting could. Falling for him would be a huge problem—for both of them. She knew first-hand how much it could hurt, how terrifying it could be to love someone. Right now, her feelings for Caleb were manageable. Safe. She didn't want that to change. She absolutely wasn't going to *ask* him to change that.

So she took a seat at the back of the boat, and watched Caleb steer them away from the dock and out towards the centre of the lake. She should really have her eyes on the landscape, she told herself. It wasn't as if she were going to find herself in a speed-boat on a private Italian lake every week. But she supposed that Caleb had put a lot of work into those arms and someone should be admiring the results of all his hard work.

She let her eyes drift from muscular arms to shoulders, down Caleb's broad back, where it narrowed to waist and hips. Which was, of course, exactly when he looked over his shoulder and caught her ogling.

He grinned at her, flicked a switch next to the steering wheel and then came to sprawl by her on the seat. 'Neat toy,' she said, not wanting his attention on the way she had just been staring at him.

'I think so. And, er, the view.'

She directed her gaze very pointedly to the mountains in the distance.

'Not too bad,' she pronounced, and Caleb laughed.

'So, do you want to swim? Or I can show you what the boat can really do or...'

'Or?' Ally asked, wondering how dis-tressed—or how tempted—she would be if he suggested something that could possibly ruin their friendship for ever.

'We could try taking some photos again for your parents?'

'Photos?' she asked, her comprehension still lagging by a few seconds.

Caleb frowned at her. 'Yes. Magical pictures you take with your phone and can send to other phones. Like the ones you planned to send to your parents to make it clear that they don't need to rebook you on your singles cruise.'

'Oh, those types of photos,' she said with a nervous smile, burying any thoughts of other sorts of photos that they could be taking out here, in the Italian sunshine, with no one around to see. The sort that she would never, *ever*, send to her parents. 'As long as you promise not to try and drown me again.'

'You're never going to let me live that down, are you?' Caleb groaned, covering his face with a hand.

'I'm not planning on it,' Ally confirmed. 'So,' she said, shuffling closer to Caleb and pulling her phone out of her shorts pocket. 'Cute couple selfies?'

She glanced up at him, but looked away when their eyes met, afraid of what it would mean if she let herself gaze into his eyes, as she was tempted to do, and pulled her sunglasses down onto her face. She rested her head on his shoulder and held her phone out for a selfie, firing off a couple of shots. Caleb reached an arm around her shoulder, pulling her into him as he took the phone from her hand. 'Longer arms,' he explained, smiling and kissing the top of her head as he took another few pictures.

This was all just for show, Ally reminded herself, not letting herself get carried away with thinking about his body pressing against hers, the warmth of his cheek on the top of her head. How easy it would be to close her eyes, relax and simply enjoy being close to him. She couldn't do that. She knew how much she could get hurt, or—worse— she could hurt Caleb, and she wasn't prepared to do that.

So when Caleb handed the phone back, she scrolled through the gallery as an objective observer. Not at all moved by the sight of them looking happy and affectionate in their photos.

'What do you think?' Caleb asked.

'Fine. They're fine.'

'I think we look like friends,' Caleb said, frowning a little.

She snorted. 'We are friends.'

'I'm just not sure that your mum will buy us being a couple. I think we could try a bit harder to be convincing, if you wanted to.'

If she wanted to? Did *he* want to? She had her suspicions about what 'trying harder' might look like, and it wasn't the sort of thing that she usually did with her friends.

'Like what?' she asked.

'Like you could take your shirt off, for a start.'

She raised her eyebrows. 'Once again, it's hard not to think that you might have an ulterior motive.' God knew she was not going to turn down the chance to see him shirtless again. *Looking* was safe enough, surely. Looking wasn't touching.

'Just take your shirt off,' he said, and she should have hated the bossy tone in his voice, but instead she found herself reaching for the hem of her top. She stopped herself a fraction of a second before she complied unthinkingly.

'I will if you will,' she challenged.

Well, that backfired, she mused as he

whipped his shirt off and managed to take a picture of her still drooling before she could pull herself together.

'That's not going to prove anything to my mum,' she reasoned. 'You're not even in the shot.'

'No, but I'm going to keep it anyway,' he said, smiling as he sent it to himself.

'Right, get down here,' Caleb said, lying back and stretching himself out on the deck of the boat. She lay down tentatively beside him, but he scooped her closer with an arm around her waist until she was lying half on top of him. His arm moved higher, until his hand met the nape of her neck, his fingers threaded through her hair and tilted her face up. He nudged her nose with his.

'This might be a bit more convincing,' he suggested, his mouth so close that his lips brushed against hers as he spoke.

She pulled together every ounce of self-control she could muster to avoid kissing the smug expression off his face. 'And if we were here, on your boat, like this, why exactly would we be taking pictures to send home to my parents?' she managed to say, praising herself as she did it for her ability to string a sentence together while distracted in the most complete possible way.

She was distantly aware of the presence of her phone while Caleb stroked strands of hair out of her face. And then of Caleb shifting them slightly, his nose crashing against hers.

'Wh—?'

'Light's better at this angle,' he said, and she couldn't believe he had the capacity to be thinking of lighting and camera angles when she was doing her best just to remember to keep her heart beating and breath going in and out of her lungs.

He rolled and the boat rocked as he landed on top of her, any chance of breathing lost completely as his hair fell into her eyes and filtered out the sunshine, isolating them in their own world. She wrapped one foot around his calf before she could think about what she was doing, and both of them froze.

'I really don't think we should be sending photos of this to my parents,' she managed to say in a shaky voice, before realising that Caleb had already dropped the camera. This wasn't for show, then. This was just the two of them, bodies as close as two people could be.

'So we should probably stop this now,' Caleb said, without any suggestion that he was going to move.

'Definitely,' she agreed.

She held her breath as he lay half on top of her for another second. And then another more. And then she remembered, this wasn't some cute guy that she had just met. This was *Caleb*. Her Caleb, and she had promised herself that she wasn't going to risk losing him over a kiss or a fling.

So she wriggled away before she could do anything stupid, the boat rocking slightly in the wake of her movement. She closed her eyes against the sun, listening to Caleb's breathing, and wondering whether she had just spoiled things.

'That was pretty convincing, then.'

'Do not send those photos to my mother,' Ally managed to say while she tried to get her breathing under control.

'Definitely not,' Caleb agreed. 'I'll delete them.'

'No!' Ally almost shouted. 'I mean, just…

Fine, yes, delete them. If that's what you want.' Caleb just handed her the phone back.

Great, something else for her list of things not to think about, she thought as she slid the phone into her pocket.

'We should do something less… NSFW,' she suggested, looking desperately for safe ground.

'I brought a pack of cards,' Caleb replied, still not properly looking at her.

'Yes. That,' Ally said with a sigh of relief, reaching into the cooler and pulling out two cans of lemonade. She cracked the first and handed it to Caleb.

They played a few hands of poker, using olives to place stakes, until the game took a back seat to simply reclining on the seats, feeling the sun on their faces and the gentle rock of the boat on the water.

The boat gave a gentle lurch, and Ally opened her eyes to see what had caused it, only to groan and snap them closed when she remembered that Caleb still had no shirt on.

'Next time we are going on holiday somewhere cold,' she declared, throwing her arm over her face for added drama.

Caleb laughed. Then, 'Next time?' he asked tentatively.

'I mean, just a holiday. Maybe. I think I'd miss your face if I never saw it again. I'm looking forward to things being normal again, but maybe once a year we can hang out like this. But with less nudity,' she suggested, with a pointed look at his bare torso.

'I hear Scandinavia is nice in the winter,' he offered.

She thought about it. 'No hot springs.'

'Deal.'

She just sat and looked at him, wondered how long she could get away with that. Before she shook her head and brought herself back to real life. 'You need sunscreen, too,' Ally said, looking critically over the skin he had on show. She held out her hand for the sunscreen, telling herself that this didn't mean anything. Being careful about sun protection was just a responsible thing to do. And Caleb's back was so broad there was no way that he could reach it all by himself.

She started with his shoulders, tucking his body between her knees as she smoothed the lotion over his shoulders, sliding her hands up to the nape of his neck and learning the shape of his muscles, the give and the slide of his skin.

As her hands moved, the tension leached from his muscles until he was languid and heavy, and she could just imagine him sinking back against her until she had no choice but to give up on the pretence of sun protection, let her arms wrap gently around him and rest her chin on the top of his head. But the longer that she thought about it, the less she could be sure that their friendship would survive it. So she flipped the lid back on the sunscreen with an audible click, making Caleb look back at her over his shoulder.

When his eyes met hers, it was as if a hook grabbed her somewhere behind her sternum and pulled. It must have been her axis that shifted. Her centre of gravity that moved. She knew on an intellectual level that it couldn't be the whole planet or the universal laws of physics that had altered when his eyes met hers. When she noticed for the first time the flecks of green in with the brown and golds, but that didn't mean that it didn't feel that way. She smoothed her thumbs over his cheekbones, telling herself that it was just because she still had the sunscreen on her hands that this was purely practical. Not because she wanted it so much that she physically could not keep her hands off him.

And then when he groaned, she felt it on every plane of her existence and on several that she was sure had yet to be discovered. He shifted around so that he could look properly at her, and one hand cupped her cheek, leaving her in no doubt what was coming next. He was going to kiss her, and she was desperate for him to do it. Which was why she couldn't let this happen. Not when she couldn't be sure that her usual defence mechanisms wouldn't snap into place.

The last thing that she wanted was to freeze him out, but she knew herself well enough to realise she didn't do it by choice. She got scared and she lashed out. Caleb didn't deserve that, especially not now she had more of an idea of how he'd been hurt by his parents leaving him. By all that his family had been through since. He had trusted her with that and she wasn't going to repay that trust by letting her own relationship issues get in the way of a friendship that was so important to her. They could fool around later once she had this wobble, or whatever it was, under control.

She shifted to put some space between them, and, as she had known that he would, he instantly took the hint and moved away. 'Shall we make a start on this picnic?'

Ally smiled, relieved and grateful to have a friend who understood her so well, with just an undercurrent of discomfort about what it meant if she was already having feelings about wanting to kiss him and not wanting to lose him. Walking away from the danger wasn't an option this time. She had to deal with them in a way that wouldn't mean closing off Caleb from her life. She would just have to compartmentalise, she told herself. The Caleb she loved as a friend in one box. The Caleb she had kissed and whose body she couldn't keep her eyes off in another.

Eating a picnic equalled Friend Caleb, which meant easy banter and not staring at his chest. She put on her sunglasses and sat up, but didn't breathe right until Caleb took pity on her and pulled on his shirt.

Caleb spread a blanket on the floor between them, and they both pulled items out of the cooler, passing cheeses and artichoke hearts and stuffed olives between them. And if their hands brushed as they both reached for the *taralli* crackers, or Caleb's tongue flickered against her finger when she insisted that he try the sun-blush tomato that had just changed her entire world, well, that was fine. She would simply file those feelings away in the 'Hot Caleb' box and carry on her increasingly perfect afternoon with Friend Caleb.

When they were sleepy and full from an excess of antipasti and Sicilian lemonade, they stretched out on the blanket in comfortable silence, and Ally had to actively resist the urge to let her fingers play across the hair on Caleb's stomach and trace it down to the waistband of his shorts. To let her fingers dip into the valleys between his abs, under his pectorals, and then measure his biceps by squeezing her hands around them. The sleepier she got, the harder it was to keep the contents of those two Caleb boxes strictly separated. She forced herself upright, resting on her elbows.

'Bored?' Caleb asked beside her, turning

to his side and propping his head up with one hand.

'Not bored, but thinking that it would be a shame to come all this way to see your speedboat and not see it doing any actual speeding.'

He grinned. 'I think I could be talked into showing you that.'

They packed away the picnic and stowed their bags then Caleb sat at the wheel while Ally perched on a seat behind him. She was leaning forwards, elbows on knees, in her eagerness, which did something so unholy to her cleavage that he had to look away before he did something that would capsize the boat.

He fixed his eyes on the water ahead of him and opened up the throttle, letting the tension in his body ease as he watched the speed climb and climb. Not letting off the throttle, he leaned on the wheel, turning them in a wide, graceful circle, keeping them on the edge of control. And when he slowed down to a steady cruise, Ally's eyes were bright and a huge grin had spread across her face. A few drops of water glistened on her hair.

'Do you want a turn?'

'Oh, my God, can I? You trust me?'

He laughed off the question, refusing to read more into it than he was sure that she had intended.

'Of course I do. Come, sit here.' He shifted so that she could sit between his thighs. Considering that their relationship was supposed to be entirely fake, and there was no one else on the boat to see them right now, there was rather more physical contact than he had been expecting.

'I'll show you the ropes,' he said, forcing himself to think about anything other than Ally scrambling into his lap, pushing his thighs wider apart, settling her hands over his on the wheel. To try not to notice the way that his forearms brushed against the sides of her breasts, that if he leaned forward and looked down he'd be able to see... He looked up at the sky and squeezed his eyes shut as a matter of urgency, trying to shift back in his seat without touching any more of Ally's sinfully tempting skin.

It took more than a few long moments before he trusted himself to speak.

'Ready?' he asked, and pushed her hand on the throttle to pick up speed. Ally squealed as he guided her hands on the wheel, taking them in a series of sharp turns that had spray catching their faces and hair. She looked back over her shoulder and met his eye, and she had droplets of water on her eyelashes, little jewels glinting in the sunshine. Her cheeks were pink, her smile lines deep, and he wanted to capture the sight in oils and pastels and watercolours. He wanted her smile and her flushed cheeks and her wide eyes immortalised on the walls of his house, so that he would see her like this wherever he looked.

That was not how he was meant to feel about his best friend. That was so much more complicated than liking hanging out with someone. Or wanting to make them laugh. Or even wanting to sleep with them.

He wiped a sheen of lake water from Ally's cheekbone with his thumb. 'I'm having second thoughts about selling the boat, if this is the expression it puts on your face.'

'Can you have it shipped home?' Ally

asked, still grinning and glowing in equal measure. 'I can see us tearing up and down the Thames in it.'

It was on the tip of his tongue to remind her that after this week they'd agreed to go back to keeping a screen between them. If she hadn't noticed her slip, and her intention to keep him in her life, then he wasn't going to be the one to remind her.

'I'll absolutely think about it,' he told her, attempting in vain to hide his smile for fear of tipping her off.

The rest of the afternoon passed in a haze of sunshine, stretching out on the loungers, passing cold drinks to one another, picking at the remains of their picnic, swapping tit-bits of gossip and not allowing their conversation to drift anywhere that might lead to a serious discussion of exactly what they were to each other.

Despite the compelling urge he seemed unable to bury to pick at the conversation they'd had in the olive grove the day before. She was so convinced that falling for someone would only lead to trouble. And, well, he could hardly take her to task on it when he was no more keen to have someone fall for him than she was to fall.

But there was still a part of him that made him want to change her mind. Made him want to ask her to give him a chance. To take a risk. But then he remembered what happened to the people who decided they cared for him, and that he had told himself that he had every much as good a reason to resist whatever was happening here as she did. They neither of them wanted to be more than friends. Nothing that had happened here, and nothing that had happened in his bed this morning, changed that. It was all part of the pretence they were playing on their families, that was all.

'What are you thinking so hard about over there?' Ally asked without opening her eyes, which made him wonder how she could possibly know that he'd been thinking about anything at all.

'Nothing,' he lied, turning onto his side and propping his head on one hand. 'Just wondering if we ought to head back.'

'We've run out of food so I won't argue.'

'We'll probably have to deal with the others.'

Ally let out something halfway between

a laugh and a sigh. 'You say that like it's an elaborate form of torture.' She rolled to her side, propped up her head, and he had no choice but to notice that she was mirroring his body language. He wouldn't let himself read anything into that. He. Would. Not. 'Dinner was fun last night.'

'I just find them hard work,' he said, deliberately not making eye contact.

'Do you think maybe you find yourself being hard work around them?' Ally asked.

'I have no idea what that means.'

'It means, whenever I've seen you with them, you put more effort into holding yourself apart from them than being involved. Perhaps if you just…relaxed and allowed it to happen, allowed them to be close to you, you wouldn't find it so hard just being with them.'

Caleb bristled, because all that was a little closer to the truth than was entirely comfortable. 'I don't do that,' he said.

'I think you do,' Ally argued. 'I think when you're faced with the choice to be a part of their lives or not, you choose not.'

'I'm on holiday with them, aren't I? Doesn't that count as being a part of their lives?'

'They invited *themselves*. And you brought a fake girlfriend to act as a buffer,' she pointed out, somewhat unfairly. 'And now we're hiding from them in the middle of a lake.'

Well, when she put it like that, it made him sound completely unreasonable. 'We aren't hiding,' Caleb protested, searching for any high ground in this argument. 'We're hanging out. Spending quality time together. It's different.'

'Then why do you look so forlorn at the idea of going back to the house?'

'I was just looking out for you!' he said, his voice raised. 'Rowan will try and make you play tennis, or Liv and Adam will want you to take sides in one of their arguments. Jonathan will start talking about balance sheets!'

Ally crossed her arms, pulled off her sunglasses so she could look him properly in the eye. 'And I'm telling you I don't need you to look out for me! I'd *like* to get to know your family. I would have done it already if you hadn't kept dragging us away from them at every opportunity!'

Caleb shook his head. She was being so

stubborn about this and she didn't understand. This wasn't her family, and she'd only
been here a day. 'We all had dinner together
last night,' he pointed out, determined not
to sound sulky.

'You were the first to leave the table!'

'Only because you fell asleep!'

'I was not asleep! And even if I had been,
it wasn't like you were devastated to have
your evening cut short. You were looking
for any excuse to leave from the moment that
we sat down!' There were frown lines on her
forehead that *he* had put there, and he wanted
to kick himself. This was meant to be a fun
trip out, and instead they were fighting about
his relationship with his family. He hated that
he did this. And he didn't know what he was
meant to do to stop it—it didn't matter who
he was close to, it always ended up like this.
With an argument, and him hating that it was
happening.

'Fine, okay, I didn't want to be there,' he
conceded at last. What was the point in arguing when Ally could see right through his
lies anyway? 'You were the only thing that
made it remotely bearable. But I couldn't

wait until we were on our own again and I could have you all to myself. Are you happy now?'

It was true. From the minute that he'd sat down at the table last night, he'd wanted nothing more than for dinner to be over. But for once that hadn't had anything to do with his family and had had everything to do with getting Ally on her own. With not having to share her or her attention or see her smiling at his family. He knew he was selfish, and that it made him sound unreasonable, but he only had this week with her and he wanted all that for himself.

She said nothing for a beat, and he wondered how badly he'd screwed up. Had he freaked her out completely? Was she going to walk away?

'Why did you want that?' she asked slowly, carefully. 'What would you do with me if you had me all to yourself?'

He drew in a deep breath, let it out slowly, trying to keep his racing heart under control. 'Because I like being with you, Ally,' he said. She deserved his honesty. He might be a screw-up, but he could at least give her the truth about that. 'Because I never stop thinking about you. Because I held you in my arms all last night and...' He trailed off, not trusting himself to finish that sentence.

Her eyes widened in surprise, and then narrowed, drifting down to focus on his lips as if she couldn't help herself. 'And?' she prompted, taking both of their lives into her hands with that one word.

'And I don't know what to do with that,' he admitted. 'I don't know what to do with the fact that I can't stop thinking about kissing you, even though the only times we've kissed it wasn't even real. Wasn't meant to be real. I don't know what to do with these feelings I'm having for you, Ally.'

Her body stiffened immediately, and she drew her knees up to wrap her arms around them. He'd gone too far, he realised instantly, and reached a hand out to reassure her, but she flinched away. 'Ally, I'm sorry. I didn't mean to say that. Pretend that I didn't say that.' But he could see the damage he was doing already. Something had closed off behind her eyes and she'd drawn herself inwards, protecting herself. Protecting herself from him.

'No, it's fine. It's nothing,' she said, but he

knew that she was lying. 'It's just confusing because we've been faking being together. You don't have real feelings for me, Caleb.'

How could he argue with her when he could see full well that it was only believing those words that was stopping her running for it? That and the fact that they were in the middle of a lake. He knew that what she wanted, needed, right now was space. He was convinced that if they weren't currently on a boat in the middle of a lake, she would have walked away already. And it was his fault that she couldn't.

'I'll take us back now,' Caleb said, and Ally faked a smile that didn't convince him in the slightest. Because she could tell him that his feelings weren't real, but he knew that wasn't true. And if Ally had believed it then she wouldn't be so freaked out right now.

'Yeah. I think that's probably a good idea,' she said, not meeting his eyes.

The speed of the boat meant that the silent, awkward journey back was at least mercifully short. He had made a mistake bringing Ally here, to Italy, and now she knew it as well as he did. He had no doubt that she would already be making plans to get away from him. He knew her usual reactions when things got emotional, and it wasn't to stick around and talk about it.

This was a disaster, Ally thought to herself. Why had Caleb decided that the right place to be honest about his feelings for once was in the middle of a lake, where the universal laws of physics made it impossible for her to run away? At least Caleb was wasting no time getting them back to the shore. He was gunning the boat every bit as fast as he had when he had been showing off to her what his toy could do.

Why had he told her that he had feelings for her? Of course she had suspected it… She hadn't missed the crazy chemistry of their practice kiss, nor the way that they had woken wrapped around one another this morning. But she had thought that they were both going to ignore it. That was the sensible thing to do, the right thing to do that wouldn't ruin their friendship. That wouldn't make her push him away because she was scared of how big her feelings for him might grow. How much they could hurt each other if they allowed that to happen.

What was the point of having a fake boyfriend if you ended up in the same arguments that you would with a real one?

Why couldn't everything just stay the same? Sure, Caleb had become more important to her than just about anyone else over the last year. And that had seemed fine, before, when they didn't see each other in person. Because how much could somebody hurt her, or how much could she hurt somebody else, if they didn't know each other in real life?

And then the fact that they *were* good friends, that was meant to stop something like this happening. They were meant to skip the flirtation stage, had gone straight into deep devoted friendship. Attraction wasn't meant to rear its head when they'd already been platonic friends for so long.

Even when they'd realised that that was what was going on, why couldn't he just ignore it as they had been doing until now? Why drag it out into the open where they had to look at it and be scared of it, forcing her to try and protect herself?

She would have to leave. She could get a taxi to the airport, and…well, even if there wasn't a flight that day, there had to be one the next. She could sleep on a bench at the airport for a night if she had to. It was no big deal. All she had to do was get herself away from Caleb to a safe distance, where she couldn't hurt anyone, or get hurt herself.

Caleb steered them alongside the jetty, tied the boat securely and disembarked. He held out his hand to help her do the same. And, oh, but it was inconvenient that it was so much harder to pretend that she was half-way home already when her hand was in his, so present and so very real. And then came the moment when he should have let her hand drop, if all he'd been doing was steadying her back onto dry ground, but he…didn't. She watched the moment when he should have done it come and go, and looked up at him, wondering what he was thinking.

'Ally, I'm really sorry. We're friends. I don't want that to change. If you want me to, I can find you a flight home because I know that must be what you're thinking about. So just give me an hour and I'll get everything sorted.'

His words stopped her thoughts in their tracks. It was exactly what she had expected to want. But now that she was here, with the keys to doing a runner in her lap, it didn't seem so appealing. He'd known that she'd want to leave. To run. And he was, what? Just okay with that? She couldn't see how if she left now they'd be able to pick up their online friendship as if this couple of days had never happened. So walking out on this argument meant walking out on all of it. The fake dating charade. The scarily real-feeling kiss. And their extremely real, extremely-important-part-of-her life friendship. Was she really willing to lose all of that because Caleb had admitted that he was, what, confused about his feelings for her? Perhaps she was overreacting. They had created a confusing scenario, after all. It made sense that some of the things that they were faking would leak into their real lives. But that didn't mean that it *was* real. Things could just go back to normal if they carried on behaving as if they already were.

'Do…do you want me to leave?' she

asked. Because maybe that would save her from trying to work out what she wanted, if his words had been a demand rather than an offer. 'No,' he said, hand in his hair again. 'No, I don't want you to leave. I just thought… I overstepped and I know you don't like to stick around when things get… intense like that. I don't want to be something that stands in the way of what you want. You deserve that, Ally.'

She took a few deep breaths, until she couldn't hear her heartbeat pounding in her ears. 'I… Thank you. I appreciate you saying that. But I want to stay. If that's okay with you.' She didn't want to examine her reaction to the grin that appeared on his face at her words. If she did that she'd have to acknowledge the cool, empty space that had been opening up in her chest as they'd headed back to shore. And then how his words had triggered the whoosh of it refilling with something warm and glowing and threatening to fill her up. 'I like hanging out with you, and I know you didn't mean what you said, so we can just carry on hanging out like you never even said it. Okay?'

'Okay,' Caleb said, his voice carefully uninflected. 'Okay,' he said again, with a little more warmth.

He didn't let go of her hand, and she didn't pull it back. The net result being that they found themselves walking along the jetty hand in hand, both of them seeming to do their best not to mention how close their friendship had just come to tearing apart, but instead of that happening, somehow they were literally hanging onto one another. They slowed, the closer they got to the villa. The closer they got to spending time with his siblings, which was what had started their argument in the first place. If he wanted to hang out just the two of them, then fine. It wasn't her job to fix whatever was going on with him and his family. She had no intention of further rocking the boat—even if only figuratively speaking—now that they had recovered from what had happened out on the water.

As they reached the terrace, she could hear familiar voices, and guessed that the others were all by the pool, and that they'd be invited to join them. She would absolutely not read anything into whether Caleb would have changed his mind as a result of their...

argument. She absolutely did not want him to change. Not least because of something that she had said. But she would like him to be happy. And she could see quite clearly that the gulf between Caleb and his family hurt him. The way that he held a part of himself back—the best part, the part that really cared—when he was with them. He was scared to lose them. That much seemed pretty clear to her. But if pointing that out resulted in them fighting, she wouldn't point it out again. It wasn't worth losing him over. No more than it was worth him turning her searching questions back on her.

Caleb's fingers tensed as they reached the terrace, and she was about to reassure him that they could go and be on their own if he wanted. But then with a tug on their linked hands he pulled away, all but towing her towards the pool.

'Caleb!' Rowan called as soon as they came into view. 'Come and play tennis. Your sister won't get off her butt and we need a fourth for doubles.'

He glanced across at Ally with a look that was pure 'I told you so' and she gave him a careful smile and squeezed his fingers in a reassuring sort of way. 'Are you going to play?' she asked.

He wanted to say no. But it was just a game of tennis, and if it pleased Ally to see him do it... He liked pleasing Ally, and it didn't cost him anything. 'Will you be okay by yourself?' he asked.

She leaned in and, after just a fraction of a second's hesitation, kissed him on the cheek. 'I'll be fine. Go and have fun.'

CHAPTER FIVE

WHAT ON EARTH did she think she was doing? Ally had to ask herself.

Caleb had given her the perfect opportunity to run headlong in the opposite direction from whatever it was that they had been circling around here, and she'd just… not taken it? It wasn't even that she'd been passive in not leaving—she had made an *active* decision to stay, even after she'd been handed the chance of a prompt flight home.

But she'd stayed—because she wanted to.

Because she was scared of what it would mean for her and Caleb's friendship if she walked away from him now.

She went to sit beside Liv on one of the sun loungers and adjusted the angle slightly—just so that the sun wouldn't be in her eyes, she told herself. Nothing at all to do with the fact that it gave her a better view of the tennis courts where Caleb and Rowan were knocking a tennis ball between them, and Ally smiled, relieved to see him trying when an hour ago he had been so tense that she wouldn't have been surprised to see him shatter in front of her. The others had gone quiet when he'd walked over to the tennis court, as if they couldn't quite believe that he'd accepted their invitation. But their surprised expressions had soon turned into grins of pleasure as they'd started to play, and Caleb had begun to ease up a little.

She couldn't make herself think about what he'd admitted to her on the boat about his feelings. But she couldn't avoid thinking about the fact that she was still here. He had offered her a way out, knowing that her instinct would be to shut him out. He had understood what she had needed without her having to say it, and had offered it to her even though it would have hurt him. But here she still was.

Perhaps the fact that she'd chosen to stay would go some way towards convincing him that he was the sort of guy who was worth sticking around for. If he decided he wanted to date someone—not her, obviously—for real one day. It was totally up to him if he wanted to choose that or not. But she couldn't leave him out in the world thinking that he was someone who she could walk away from without a backward glance. He deserved to know—to believe—that he was worth more than that. It was just her job as a friend to keep showing him that, again and again if need be.

His friend.

A friend would take an interest in how his tennis match was going, she told her herself, as her eyes followed the ripples in the muscles of his arm as he easily returned the ball across the court.

'He's one of those annoying people who are just good at stuff, isn't he?' she huffed in Liv's direction.

Liv lifted her sunglasses and shot her a sideways glance. 'Well, until a couple of days ago I wouldn't have said so. But then you come along and it turns out he's been keeping all kinds of secrets all along.'

'I didn't realise I was a secret,' Ally confessed.

'We didn't realise my brother was such a dark horse,' Liv said with a wry smile.

Should she be upset that Caleb apparently hadn't said a word about her to his family? Ally wondered. Not once, in the year since they had first met online. It would probably be more of a worry if she hadn't seen for herself how actively he avoided even the company of his siblings, never mind talking with them about someone who was important to him. Even with everything that she was unsure about, the fact that she was important to him—there somehow wasn't any doubt in her mind about that—even if his sister hadn't known that she'd existed two days ago wasn't enough to change her belief.

'Don't let him push you away,' Liv said, looking serious for the first time since Ally had met her. 'We've all been trying to get through to him. It's the reason we invited ourselves here in the first place. But he doesn't listen to us when we tell him we want him around. Apparently he pays more attention to you. I'm glad he's got you,' Liv added, letting her sunglasses fall back down. 'He seems happier.'

Ally let out a long breath, slotting puzzle pieces together and trying to work out how they added up to a Caleb. 'Yeah, I'm not sure that he'd agree with that right now.'

Liv scoffed. 'What? Did you have a fight? Every couple fights sometimes. Me and Adam haven't properly started our day until we're three arguments deep. Caleb'll try to push you away—I'm warning you. If you care about him, don't let him do it, okay?'

If Ally had had any doubts about whether staying was the right thing to do, as she looked back at the doubles match, they fled. If she couldn't stay for herself, she could do it to make sure that Caleb knew that he was exactly the kind of person that people around him wanted in their life.

That when he cut people off, he wasn't protecting them, he was hurting them. The thought gave her a stab of guilt, thinking of all the perfectly nice men that she'd shut out of her own life over the years. How many of them had been hurt when she'd laid down her rigid boundaries?

But just because Caleb was guilty of flawed thinking didn't mean that she was as well. After all, the only person she was trying to protect was herself. And, yes, she was aware of how selfish that sounded, but she'd spent a large portion of her life with every choice and action taken out of her control. Why shouldn't she be selfish, now that she actually had choices about what happened in her life rather than having it dictated to her by her doctors and her parents? Just because she questioned whether Caleb was hurting himself with his choices didn't mean that she was doing the same.

She tried to concentrate her mind on the tennis match to try and quiet the sense that she wasn't being entirely honest with herself. Caleb had once again sacrificed his shirt to the heat of the afternoon, which led her to believe that this temperature, whatever it happened to be, was her ideal weather. The beads of sweat that were trickling down his spine were only further evidence of this, whatever she'd said on the boat about going somewhere cold next time.

Caleb glanced over just as she was wondering how creepy she was to be practically salivating over his sweat. She at least had her sunglasses down to hide the flame emojis that she was certain were flickering in her pupils at that moment, though she was sure from the smug grin that appeared on his face that her general appreciation for the scene had been apparent enough. How was she meant to survive five more days of him looking at her like that without her emotions doing something stupid in Caleb's direction? Five days were frightening enough. The nights were another question entirely… They couldn't count on her practically falling asleep at the table again to ensure that they made sensible decisions after they retired to their bedroom for the night.

She hadn't been good in her adult life at denying herself the things that she wanted. Why not, when she had missed out on so much earlier in her life? But she was also used to having ultimate control over the consequences of her choices, and she knew in that moment—without a doubt—that wouldn't be the case here.

If she slept with Caleb, well, if she did more than sleep with him, she would no longer have control over their relationship. She couldn't—wouldn't—hurt Caleb by shutting him out, but if she wasn't willing to do that, then how would she be able to stop herself getting hurt? She sat up abruptly when she realised that the sporty types had finished their game while she had been performing mental gymnastics. Caleb came over and collapsed at the end of her lounger.

'Remind me never to do anything competitive with Rowan ever again,' he gasped, his hand over his eyes to shield them from the sun.

'Aw, poor baby,' she said, remembering that, whatever had happened between them on the boat, she was meant to be playing the part of the adoring girlfriend. She combed her hands through his damp hair, trying not to think too hard about how much of this easy intimacy was their real friendship, and how much was the fake relationship that she was going to lose at the end of this week. She pulled her hand away at the thought, but Caleb caught her wrist and brought it back until it was tangled tightly in his hair again. 'That feels nice,' he muttered as she pressed her fingers into his scalp.

She reached for her glass of water and nudged him with her knee until he opened one eye and looked up at her. She let a couple of drops of condensation snake down the side of the glass, linger on the rim at the bottom, and then drop onto his overheated skin. Caleb pushed himself up onto his elbows and looked at the glass of water as if he had just trekked across a desert.

'I would do terrible, terrible things for a sip of that water,' he told her, his voice low and rough. 'You can name your price.'

Ally raised one eyebrow and smiled as she considered what she would ask for. A kiss was the obvious answer in a situation like this, but she was already entitled to those as his fake girlfriend. She wasn't going to waste it.

'You can have it on credit,' she said, smiling wryly as she handed him the glass. 'I'll set my price later.'

'I don't know—what if I don't like the price?' Caleb asked, regarding her suspiciously.

She shrugged—that was so not her problem. 'I don't know…' she repeated sardonically. 'I suppose it depends on how badly you want the water.'

He sat up and gave her a meaningful look, not even breaking eye contact as he took one long gulp of the water after another until the glass was empty. Ally raised her eyebrows, refusing to smile, to rise to his provocation.

She liked this playful Caleb, wondered how she could keep him for longer. 'I thought it was a favour for a sip,' she observed as he collapsed back beside her thighs. 'You drank the whole glass.'

He smirked, closing his eyes. 'You don't scare me.'

She laughed, giving up the pretence of being serious. 'You *should* be afraid,' she told him. 'Don't think I won't make you pay up.'

That only broadened his smirk into a smile. 'I can't wait.'

Her whole body warmed at the thought of the favours she could call in later that night. For a moment, her brain short-circuited, overwhelmed by the possibilities unravelling before her. The only option her brain didn't consider was the one that they'd planned from the start: a chaste night with no sex.

She looked down at Caleb and wished she could read his mind. He had said that he had wanted her all to himself the night before. Did he still feel that way? What might have happened if she hadn't sparked out on him the moment that her head had hit the pillow?

And they hadn't discussed sleeping arrangements for tonight. He *had* held her all of last night, and she had let him. Could she risk letting him do that again? Risk letting him do more than that?

'Jonathan's going to light the pizza oven!' Rowan called from somewhere behind them. Ally let a small smile catch the corner of her lip and nudged at Caleb's side with her knee again, inspiration striking. 'Hey. Get up, I'm cashing in a favour.'

She saw the flash of heat in his face before she caught him with a hand on his chest.

'Go help your brother,' she said before he could get any ideas, and his smile instantly dropped.

'You have carte blanche to ask me for anything. *Anything*,' he reminded her with a meaningful stare. 'And you're choosing to ask me to hang out with my brother?'

Ally took a deep breath, committing to this, despite the clear temptation that he was offering. Some things were more important. She had to make him see how much he was cared for. Loved. Even if it made him angry with her. He was worth it. His happiness was worth it.

'You agreed to anything and this is what I choose,' she told him firmly. 'If you manage to look like you're enjoying it I'll knock two credits off your account.'

He gave her a stern, hard look, and the degree to which he was fighting this only made her trust her instincts even more. After all, she wasn't forcing him. This was just a game. A way to nudge him towards something he needed. A way for him to take something he wanted without admitting it—to himself or to anyone else.

He gave her a final scowl as he got up, but she felt something warm and glowing in her chest as she looked over her shoulder and saw Caleb in stilted conversation with Jonathan. It wasn't happy families. Not yet, but it was a start. And at dinner, she had to hide a smile as she watched him get drawn into conversations with his brother, his sister, with Rowan and Adam too. Could see the surprise and pleasure in their faces. When she finished her glass of wine and decided she couldn't possibly manage another slice of pizza, she could see the fatigue and strain on Caleb's face.

'I'm ready to turn in,' she said softly, leaning into him.

He let out a long breath. 'Yeah, me too,' he said, his body relaxing in front of her eyes. He slipped his hand into hers as they wished everyone goodnight, and she squeezed it tightly as they walked across the terrace, reminding herself all the time that this was just for show.

How long did she have to decide what she wanted? she wondered, as they headed to the door of their room. Did it even matter? She had shot Caleb down earlier when he'd tried to talk about his feelings. Maybe she was out of chances to work out what she wanted this friendship to be. She caught her breath as she looked up and met Caleb's eye. He was looking at her as if he wanted to devour her—could she cash in her credits in order to make that happen? How many sips of water had been in that glass? How many favours could she claim?

Caleb reached for her other hand and pulled her close.

'Thank you,' he said, stepping in closer so that the front of her body was brushing up against him. It was just a hug, she told herself. Friends hugged all the time. This didn't mean anything more than his hand on hers had done.

'I thought you'd be angry with me for meddling,' she admitted, tipping her face up more to him.

'Oh, I'm angry. That was a mean trick. I intend to get my revenge.'

He caught her chin with his thumb and finger, holding it still so that she couldn't look away from the intensity of how he was looking at her.

'What sort of revenge did you have in mind?' she asked, barely risking a breath. Because this was more than friendly, and there was no one else here, so it couldn't be for show. No, the way that Caleb was looking at her right now was for no one else but her.

'I could be creative. Really make you suffer.'

A quirk at the corner of his mouth gave away that he wasn't entirely serious, but if playing along meant that he would keep looking at her like that, would keep his hand on her cheek in the way that was making her skin sing, she would go along with it.

'What if I said that I was very, very sorry?' she asked, catching one side of her lower lip between her teeth. Caleb pulled on her lip with the gentlest of pressure, and then leaned in to press his mouth to where she had bitten.

When he leaned back, she felt her head swim, held tighter with the hand still trapped in Caleb's, and leaned more into his chest to steady herself.

'That would be a start,' Caleb said, turning her head so that he could kiss the other side of her face. He had kissed her. Caleb had kissed her. And there wasn't any way that they could pretend that this was about anything other than the fact that they liked each other. They had liked each other for such a long time, and now they were here, both of them, together, and his skin on hers made her body sing, and she didn't know if she was too scared to want this or to lose it.

Caleb pulled her gently backwards by the hand, right across the room until the bed was at the back of his knees, and he sat back, leaving her standing in front of him, tucked between his thighs.

'Not going to fall asleep on me tonight?'

Caleb asked, but she knew that he was asking more than that.

'Not feeling very sleepy all of a sudden,' she admitted, and she was rewarded with a huge, unguarded grin as Caleb's arms came around her and pulled her even closer. It was nice having him look up at her for a change. Especially when he was looking at her like *this*, as if he adored her.

She should want to run from that. Should be worrying about what it meant that he had those sorts of feelings for her. But really, all she wanted was to bask in it. It had been so long since she had been the centre of someone's world for a *good* reason. Since someone was treasuring their time with her for the pure joy of her being there, rather than stacking up memories in case she didn't make it through the next week, or month, or year.

She leaned down to kiss him, keeping it light. Not wanting to rush. This wasn't anything they hadn't done before. This couldn't scare her. She was quite happy just looking down at Caleb in the lamp light casting a soft glow in the room. To learn the pattern of the freckles appearing on his cheekbones. The soft curl at his hairline where strands had escaped the elastic that kept his hair off his face. To touch his lower lip with her thumb, learning the creases, and the dip in the centre that made it look so soft and plump. She kissed him there, and then the corner of his mouth. The curve in his top lip. The place where soft skin met the scrape of stubble on his cheek.

His eyes had closed, his head tipped back, letting her take the lead. Making no demands, refusing to rush her.

She traced the long line of his jaw. Scraped gently over his Adam's apple with her fingernail. Down into the open V of his shirt until she reached the first button and flicked it open.

He took over from there, swiftly undoing buttons until his shirt lay open, and she was able to follow his fingers with her mouth, until standing was impossible even if her legs had been able to hold her up, and it made much more sense to kneel between his thighs. His eyes didn't leave hers for a second. Not as she pushed the shirt off his shoulders or reached for his belt buckle. His hands threaded through her hair as he pulled her up to meet his mouth in a hard, demanding kiss. His other arm clamped around her waist, holding her firmly against his bare chest. And then he was lifting her up, and over and around until somehow they were both flat on the bed, his arm still making clear that he wasn't letting her go, his mouth making clear she could take absolutely anything she wanted from him.

If this was his idea of a punishment, she didn't have much incentive to behave herself.

'Are you sure?' he asked, minutes, hours, days later, as she pulled him into the cradle of her thighs. 'You want this?'

The words slipped out, too honest, too revealing, but she nodded as she moaned, as she pulled him into her body. 'I want you,' she said, her words ending on a gasp as he filled her, as he rested his forehead against hers, his eyes closing as if it was all too much. She kissed his eyelids, first one side, then the other.

'Caleb, sweetheart...' The word just slipped out, she couldn't help it.

He groaned, opened his eyes, finally looked at her.

'This is…' he said, his eyes rolling, his words trailing off as he started to move inside her. 'I didn't think that it would… I couldn't imagine…' His head dropped to hers again. She ran her hands gently up his back, from the dimples at the bottom of his spine until her hand was cupped around the nape of his neck. She wanted to tell him that it was okay. That she hadn't imagined it would be like this either. But when she opened her mouth to tell him all that, all that came out was a little cry, and his mouth found hers, swallowing the sounds.

And she knew that he understood. Knew from the urgency she saw when she met his gaze. From the staccato rhythm of his body against hers. From the way that he threaded his fingers through hers and gripped her hand hard that they wouldn't be able to forget this. That whatever lies they had told themselves and each other in the safe light of day—this couldn't be undone. They couldn't pretend that this hadn't happened and go back to how they had been before.

She buried her face in his throat, tasting the salt of his sweat, drinking in the smell of woodsmoke from the tips of his hair. 'It's okay,' she whispered, not sure whether the words were meant for him or for herself. 'I've got you,' she said, when he shook in her arms. And then there were no more words. She didn't need them. Not when she could open her eyes and see everything that he felt for her in his features, when she could show him everything that she felt for him with her hands and her mouth and her body.

And after, when his heavy weight still pinned her to the mattress, and she stroked her hands through his hair, she knew that this had changed everything. And when they woke up in the morning, they were going to have to choose what this was. Who they were to each other. They couldn't carry on pretending any more that this week was something that they could play at and then go back to normal.

Ally woke up slowly, light filtering past the blinds, memories filtering through her sleepy fog. And when she remembered what they had done, she squeezed her eyes shut. Perhaps if she just refused to remember what it had been like to make love to Caleb, she could pretend that it hadn't happened. That they hadn't irrevocably changed the nature of their friendship, the only one she had that meant anything to her.

But she'd obviously been thinking loud enough to wake Caleb, and she felt him moving behind her. She pulled the sheets up to under her chin and turned over.

'Morning,' she said, forcing a smile that she was sure looked more like a grimace. He looked at her warily. Was this broken already? Was he going to make her talk about what they both felt last night and admit that she—?

'Shall we go sightseeing today?' he asked, and she could have kissed him for the reprieve if that wouldn't have been the worst idea she could possibly have come up with. Maybe they could just pretend that everything was normal. She'd been sure, with a sense of doomed certainty, when she'd gone to sleep last night that they'd ruined their friendship with no way back. But perhaps she'd been overreacting. It was probably the wine and the hormones and, well, the sex, that had made her feel that way. Perhaps, with sunshine to wash all that away, it would turn out that it had been very nice, but perfectly ordinary sex, and they could carry on just as before.

'I'd like that,' she said, playing along with the whole *normality* thing. 'Where were you thinking?'

'The nearest town's about twenty kilometres away. It's quite small but there are some Roman ruins. About a dozen churches. A few nice restaurants. It's not Rome or Venice, but...'

'No, that sounds lovely,' Ally said, venturing a real smile. Letting out her first proper breath since she had woken up and letting some of the tension go from her body.

Maybe she *had* just imagined it. Invented a whole drama when there was no need. It had probably just been a relief for both of them after a long dry spell and she'd misinterpreted it as some life-changing experience. Caleb was obviously not giving it a second thought. Thank God.

She was about to get up and get dressed when she remembered that she was wearing absolutely nothing under this sheet and, fake girlfriend or not, a girl sometimes needed a little privacy. She sat, clutching the sheet to her, and gave Caleb a meaningful look. 'If you don't mind?' she said pointedly, and he turned away as she slipped from the bed and pulled a robe from the wardrobe.

'I'm decent,' she told him, tying the belt at her waist and making sure it wasn't gaping too inappropriately at her cleavage. 'I'm going to jump in the shower,' she told him. Doing her best not to look him in the eye.

'I'll, um, start breakfast,' Caleb offered, and she darted into the bathroom before either of them could say anything that wasn't utterly mundane.

Caleb drove them into the centre of the town, through several terrifying junctions that explained why she hadn't seen a single undented car since she had left the airport. She felt as if she hadn't breathed out since they'd entered the city limits until Caleb pulled into a parking space and shut off the engine.

'Promise me I never have to drive here,' she begged, turning to Caleb with wide eyes. He laughed, and she watched him carefully to see if his good humour reached his eyes. He'd been concentrating on the road all the way here, she told herself, and she was glad of it. There was no way that she'd have wanted to do that drive with him distracted. But even now that they were stationary, when she looked over at him there was something...guarded in his expression.

Well, she wasn't going to ask him about it. It was good that he was on his guard. She was too. They both needed to be after what had happened the night before. Guarded was safe. Guarded meant not doing something stupid just because they'd got carried away.

'I promise you never have to drive here,' Caleb said, opening his door as far as it would go in the tiny space and contorting himself out of the car. Ally did the same on her side and grabbed her bag from the boot, pulling on a wide-brimmed straw hat for good measure.

Right, because it wasn't as if she would be coming back.

'What do you want to see first?' Caleb asked as they followed the signs to the centre of the town.

'Roman ruins?' Ally suggested. 'If they're outdoors we should make the most of the cool morning.' Because they'd neither of them wanted to linger in the vicinity of a bed, so they had been up and out of the house before any of the others had even stirred.

'Ruins, coffee, churches, lunch?' Caleb suggested, and Ally nodded.

'Perfetto.'

They strolled through the town until they reached the ruins, which had been excavated in one corner of the main piazza. She spent a while reading the information boards, aware of Caleb doing the same in her peripheral vision. Was she never going to be able to look at him directly again? she wondered. They'd pretended that nothing had happened when they'd first woken up, but the longer the morning went on, the more she realised that they were both pretending. She couldn't put her finger on what was giving them away, only that the ease of conversation that they usually had was gone, replaced by something more stilted and awkward. Whereas before they'd been easy looking at each other, now it was all sideways glances and quickly looking away when one or the other of them got caught at it.

It would be fine, again, after this week, she promised herself. This wouldn't last for ever. Once they were back home, she wouldn't have to see him, smell him, remember how his skin felt against hers. How he had trembled in her arms last night. How she'd come apart in his. If they could just avoid looking at each other for the next few days, perhaps they could still rescue this. Because however awkward this morning after might be, it wasn't worth losing their friendship over. It was clearer than ever that that wasn't something that she was going to be able to let go—she couldn't imagine her life without him in it, at least in some way.

She glanced across, relieved to find that he wasn't doing the same this time.

'Shall we go and explore?' she asked, and for a moment she thought Caleb was going to reach for her hand as he agreed. But he snatched it back at the last moment, and she took herself out of reach just to be sure. She jumped down into the amphitheatre, walking the sweeping arcs of the seating, trying to absorb the knowledge that they had been built nearly two thousand years ago, and were still in use today. She couldn't make her brain compute those sorts of time spans, and when it grew tired of trying she sat down, pressed her palms into the stone and tried absorbing some of their magic.

'It's hard to get your head around,' Caleb said, coming and sitting beside her, his posture a mirror of his own. His fingers close enough that she could brush her little finger against his without even having to think about it. But she resisted, because she was honestly scared of what would happen if she didn't. If she let herself have that, that tiny brush of skin on skin, where would she draw the next line, and how long would it take her to slink across it?

Caleb looked down at their hands, too, and pulled his away.

CHAPTER SIX

SHE WAS ACTING as if everything was fine—
but Caleb knew that nothing could be further from the truth. Last night had changed
everything, Ally had seen how he really
felt and that had terrified her. He'd seen it
in her eyes yesterday afternoon, and again
this morning when she'd woken up and panicked. And the only way forward that he
could see that would stop her from running
was to pretend that everything was fine.
That something in him hadn't changed for
ever last night.

He'd had plenty of sex before, and it hadn't
been anything like that. It hadn't stripped
him down and left him utterly vulnerable,
utterly revealed. And Ally had seen it. He
knew that she had, because why else would
she panic? He had shown her everything,
and she wanted to run away from him. He

knew her too well to think otherwise. He'd known this happened when other people had got too close to her.

So he was going to lie and pretend that it hadn't meant anything. Because anything else was unfair on Ally. It was burdening her with his feelings—ones that she had made absolutely clear that she didn't want to be responsible for. And he absolutely, definitely wasn't going to talk about what they'd done.

'They still put on performances here,' he said, remembering something that he'd read on the information board.

'Maybe next time—' Ally started, before stopping herself. Because, no... Of course there wasn't going to be a next time. 'You're selling the villa, so I guess you won't be coming back here either.'

Or perhaps her every waking thought wasn't about him, after all, Caleb told himself wryly. 'Yeah. I guess not. I wish I'd thought about it in advance. I could have booked something.'

The silence stretched awkwardly between them, and Caleb wondered whether a friendship like theirs had ever recovered from ill-advised sex before, or whether this was it for them now.

'Come on, you promised me coffee,' Ally said, standing abruptly and heading for the café across the piazza. She snagged one of the tables right on the edge of the piazza and had ordered coffees in beginner's Italian from the waiter by the time that he reached her.

'Quick work,' he said with a smile, and a head tilt towards the waiter. 'I didn't know that you spoke Italian.'

'I've been listening to podcasts,' she said with a shrug. 'I've barely had a chance to practise.'

'I'm sorry,' Caleb said, feeling suddenly guilty. 'I've not been a good host, have I? We've barely left the villa.'

But she smiled at him indulgently, and he tried to remind himself that he didn't get to keep that expression. That nothing this week was real. Because if he had been a different person, with a different history, he would have loved her looking at him like that. But he couldn't quite shake the knowledge that with a look like that came the potential for him to totally mess it up. For loving him to become a burden that she wasn't prepared to bear. She deserved better than that. Had survived to live whatever life she chose, not being stuck with him because he'd let his feelings for her run out of control.

'When the villa comes with a pool and an olive grove and a speedboat, I don't think there's really anything to apologise for,' Ally pointed out with another smile. 'Anyway, I didn't come here for any of that. Or to speak Italian to waiters, for that matter. I came here to spend time with you.'

And it hit him right in the chest when she said something like that. So easily expressed, that she wanted to spend time with him. But that wouldn't last—and when that pleasure in being together turned into a feeling of obligation, he didn't want to have to see it.

'I think you're here because you wanted to get out of that singles cruise,' he reminded her with a wry smile, deflecting.

She nodded, but her expression had fallen. 'And to get out of the singles cruise. Speaking of…' She pulled her phone out of her bag. 'We're meant to be sending photos to my parents, remember? So far the only ones we have either look like you're trying to drown me or aren't exactly suitable to share with family members.'

Caleb forced himself to smile as they snapped a couple of selfies, but the results looked as strained as he had felt taking them. How could they be *this* awkward after how close they had been the night before?

Well, that was a question with a simple answer. Because neither of them could afford to show what they were really feeling today. If he let Ally see how much last night had meant to him, she would be out of here faster than he could call her back. If there was even the slightest chance that she was feeling the same way about him then he knew that his instincts would be telling him to do the same. So here they were. Pretending that it hadn't mattered. That it was just something that they'd done to blow off steam, for fun. Rather than it being something that he suspected had changed the path of their friendship for ever.

But if they could just survive this week. Put some space and a screen between them so that there would be no temptation to do anything like it again, maybe they could get back to where they had been before she had arrived here.

Was that what he wanted?

'What are you thinking about?' Ally asked, after she had taken a sip of her coffee and let out a sigh that was a little too reminiscent of the night before to be decent in public.

'Nothing,' he lied. And then wished he'd come up with anything—*anything*—to say, because then perhaps there'd be even the tiniest chance that she wouldn't just assume that he was thinking about the night before.

She smiled at him, but she wasn't fooling him.

'Let's have dinner here tonight,' he said out of nowhere, and he wasn't sure if it was an olive branch, an apology, or a hope for the future. But once he'd said the words he couldn't take them back. He just knew that he had to do something different. It seemed impossible that the night before would change nothing. *Could* change anything.

'Here?' Ally said, over the rim of her coffee cup.

He tried to keep his expression neutral, shrugging slightly. 'Doesn't have to be *here*

here. Just, let's eat in the town tonight, rather than with my family.'

Ally looked at him, and he knew she was trying to calculate the implications of what he was suggesting. He held up his hands in a show of innocence. 'We don't have to, but—'

'No, I'd like that,' she said quickly, as if she was afraid that she was going to change her mind.

'Are we going to talk about last night?' he asked suddenly. Once the words were out of his mouth, he would have done anything to pull them back, but short of inventing time travel there was nothing to be done now but ride it out. To watch her facial expressions and try and work out what she was feeling.

'Do *you* want to talk about it?' Ally asked, her expression so guarded that he couldn't tell whether that was an invitation or a 'back the hell off'.

'I don't know. It just feels strange that we're not,' he admitted. 'We're both carrying on as if nothing happened. As if nothing has changed.'

She leaned forward and rested her elbows on the edge of the table, cupping her chin in her hand. 'Has something changed?'

'You don't think it has?' he asked.

She shook her head. 'I didn't say that. I just want to know what you were going to say…'

'…before you tell me what you're thinking. That hardly seems fair.' She'd sat back now, arms crossed over her chest. Putting space between them.

'Well, short of us both speaking at exactly the same time, one of us has to go first,' she pointed out.

Caleb took a breath. She was right. One of them had to do this, and unless he wanted to continue to spend this week trying to guess what she was feeling rather than talk about it, he had to show that he was willing to do this, too, and talk. 'Okay, fine,' he said. 'I'll go first. Last night was…nice.'

Ally choked on her coffee, which was fair, he supposed, given the weakness of his words. Saying 'nice' was worse than saying nothing at all. He tried again. 'It wasn't what I was expecting it to be. It was…more.'

She seemed to have recovered her composure enough to swallow her coffee, and he supposed that was something to be grateful for. Even if this conversation wasn't exactly going to plan.

'More…in what way?' she asked. He hadn't counted on this conversation being entirely one way. Was terrified that any minute she was going to decide that he'd said too much and decide to leave. But surely she wouldn't be asking if she didn't want to know how he felt?

'I don't know. I thought it would be…nice, like I said. That it would be something that we'd just done because we were here and we like one another and I think you're beautiful. I didn't expect to get so…emotional about it.'

'Nor did I,' Ally admitted.

Caleb looked up and met her eye in surprise, because the last thing that he'd been expecting from her was that sort of honesty. Why wasn't she packing her bags and putting space between them? He knew that the last thing that she'd wanted out of this week was the sort of romantic entanglement that she'd been specifically avoiding for years. What did it mean that she was willing to talk about this now?

'It was like everything about us,' Ally continued. 'It felt like you understood me in a way that no one has before. And adding sex into the mix…it was a lot. Overwhelming.'

She leaned in towards him again, and that little bit of proximity made it easier for him to breathe somehow. 'And maybe that's why you pretended it didn't happen?' he asked.

'I didn't do that!' Ally protested.

Caleb raised his eyebrows in challenge, and she softened a little, as if thinking over what she'd just said.

'Okay! Yes, I tried to be normal,' she admitted. 'I didn't want it to spoil things.'

'It will only spoil things if we let it,' he said gently, hoping that if they both believed that they could make it true. 'We can talk about it if that feels right. If we want to.'

'What is there to say about it?' Ally asked with a slight note of desperation in her voice.

'Well, did you like it?' Caleb asked.

Ally laughed, and he felt it in his chest. 'What sort of question is that?' she asked. 'I mean, if you don't know the answer to that then there's no help for us. Of course I liked it. What I didn't like was waking up this morning knowing that things had changed between us. I don't like having to try and guess what you're thinking—I'm not used to that. I've never had to think about what I was saying to you before. I always just said exactly what I was thinking. I don't like things not feeling natural between us. I don't like worrying what this means for us.'

He reached for her hand, which might have been crossing a line, but it was a chance he was willing to take if it helped with the doubt that he could see written on her face. He'd say anything to smooth the lines on her forehead that showed how unhappy she was. 'You know that you're important to me. Last night hasn't changed that, even if it doesn't happen again.'

She pulled her hand back and he instantly regretted his words.

'You don't want it to happen again?' she said in carefully measured tones.

Caleb closed his eyes, rested his head in his hands. 'I know you, Ally. Don't forget that. I know what happens when someone tries to get close. You don't like having relationships and I'm not here to try and talk you into one, not if it means losing you.'

'Okay.' She nodded. 'You're right. It was…it was lovely. But I don't want a relationship, and letting it happen again would just complicate things even more.'

Caleb shook his head, because this conversation wasn't going the way that he wanted, but anything he said to try and fix it seemed to make it worse. They were friends who had discovered that something really good happened when they slept together. And he didn't want that to mean that anything changed between them. Perhaps if she hadn't made it clear that at the first sign of anything resembling feelings she was going to freak out and leave, then he might have had something different to say this morning. But she had got up and pretended that it had never happened and so he'd moderated his feelings, kept things safe, and somehow still hurt her.

CHAPTER SEVEN

GOD, THIS WAS exactly why she didn't do this, Ally thought as they finished their coffees in silence. Because she had a pretty good idea of what Caleb was feeling this morning. Probably something pretty similar to what she herself was feeling. And that could only be bad news. Because what she was feeling was that last night had been like nothing she'd ever experienced before. Something that had filled her with joy and hope and expectation. And every single one of those feelings made her want to run.

Caleb had looked at her last night as if no one else in the universe had existed. And she hadn't even hated it—had been too far out of it at the time for it to trigger her flight response. There wasn't a fight option, or even freeze, for her. It had always been flight—she'd spent her adult life running from making these sorts of connections. But she couldn't run away from Caleb. If she was going to, she would have done it yesterday after the argument on the boat, when he'd offered to book her a flight. But she'd stayed because she knew that it was what he needed, what he deserved. And then his sister had told her that he would try and push her away, tried to push everyone away, and that it was hurting him.

So she'd put his feelings first, doubled down on her decision to stay, and it had only made everything worse.

'What was next on our plan?' she asked, their coffee long finished, ten minutes of avoiding eye contact not magically fixing the cracks in their friendship.

'Churches,' Caleb said, glancing at her, letting his gaze slide away as soon as she looked back.

'Plural?'

He nodded. 'Yeah. There's a dozen, I think. There's a trail and everything.'

She raised her eyebrows at him. 'You like churches?'

'I don't know. I like these ones, and you'll

get to see the most beautiful parts of the town.'

'Show me,' she said, risking a small smile at him as she stood up and swung her bag over her shoulder.

They walked across the square to what Caleb had told her was the first church on the trail, an imposing baroque building with a large circular window high above the door. She stood at the base of the walls and looked directly up, shading her eyes from the sun and its blinding reflection on the near-white stone. She wasn't sure how long she would have stayed there, marvelling over the intricate carvings, the details around the windows, the towering height of the columns, if Caleb hadn't interrupted her.

'Come on,' he said, taking hold of her hand and leading the way up the wide shallow steps to an enormous doorway. Ally wandered into the church, pulling a cardigan over her shoulders and rubbing her arms at the abrupt change in temperature. And then her eyes caught on the beautifully decorated columns flanking the aisle, and her gaze was guided upwards, to a window bright with light above an altar blazing with candles.

She stopped, overwhelmed by the sight, the scale. Candles hanging in chandeliers between each column and flowers festooning the ends of the pews nearest the altar.

She turned to look behind her, at the enormous rose window above the door where they had walked in, and caught her breath, the sight of it stopping her in her tracks.

Light flooded through its concentric circles, creating a starburst effect that fixed her feet to the floor and had her feeling her heart beating hard in her chest. She could feel Caleb behind her and swayed into him. His arm came around her waist and she didn't push him away. Didn't say a word. Instead she soaked in his presence in the same way that she did the light from this window. Overwhelmed by something so much larger than herself that she could barely understand it.

Caleb let his chin come down to rest on her head, and she point-blank refused to read anything into it when his other arm came round her waist as well. This was just something nice. Something that she could enjoy for its niceness, and she wasn't going to ruin it by doing something as stupid as *thinking* about it. When they eventually pulled themselves away from the window, they made their way around the church, looking at the paintings of the stations of the cross, lighting candles at the altars and in the chapels. Stopping in front of the altar to look back again up at the window. As entranced by its light as they had been the first time that they'd seen it.

Stepping back into the sunshine outside felt like re-entering the world after falling through a fissure into an alternate universe. The sun was hotter than it had been when they'd gone inside, and Ally pulled off her cardigan, and dropped her sunglasses over her eyes. 'Good luck following that,' she said with a smile at Caleb, who was just behind her, doing something with his phone.

He pulled her back to him with a hand on her hip and held out his phone in front of them both, taking a selfie with the church in the background.

Ally was looking up at him, her expression soft and affectionate, still slightly dazed from the otherworldliness of their walk around the church.

'If we send that to my mother she'll be

expecting me to come home engaged,' Ally said softly, unguardedly, unable to look away from the picture. Caleb had captured something between them that she couldn't quite put her finger on, but that made her nervous and excited in equal measure.

Caleb shrugged and posted it to the group chat that she'd set up with her mother for this purpose and kissed her softly on the cheek. 'We'll worry about that when we get home,' he said easily, and his mention of home made her think of something quite different from the life she had left, where home was her alone in a flat, with Caleb on the other end of her messaging app.

Something about being in the quiet and stillness of the church had made them soft with each other. Smoothed over the fractiousness that had threatened to derail their coffee, and when, as they followed the map to the next church on the trail, their hands brushed together, they reached for each other, rather than flinching away. After everything that they had said to each other since they had arrived in Italy, especially everything they had said to one another that morning, neither of them should have reached for the other. Threaded their fingers through the other's, clasped onto their hands as an anchor in all the uncertainties swirling about them.

Remarkably, the next church was more beautiful than the first, and the one after that more beautiful still. By the time that they were ready to stop for lunch, they'd seen every historical church within walking distance. Lit dozens of candles and managed a few more selfies to send back to her parents—hopefully enough to convince them that Caleb had taken her very much off the market, if not quite up the aisle yet.

And Caleb's arm around her shoulder had come to feel as comfortable a presence as he had been in her life for this last year. Doing that should have made things more complicated, but that didn't matter because she couldn't help herself. Was equally sure that if Caleb had been physically capable of stopping himself he would have done so.

All there was left to do was trust that they would find their way through this. That the foundations that they had built over the last year—the urgent texts and the pointless ones, the long, middle-of-the-night conversations and their quick over-a-coffee catch-ups—would help them find their way. It wasn't as if there was anyone other than Caleb that she could talk to about something like this. He had been her best friend for months. Understood her better than anyone. She'd explained what she'd been through with her family, what she was still going through with them. He knew about her dates and that she'd pushed away perfectly lovely men, and was still here, taking a risk on her, knowing that it would be hard. That there was a risk that she would hurt him too.

She squeezed closer into his side, not really thinking about it, just grateful to still have her friend, despite their mutual efforts to complicate things. He glanced across at her, and for the first time since last night, she didn't look away. Just imagined what things would be like for them if they could be so uncomplicated. That she could look at him just because she liked him. And he could look back at her, as he was now, as if she was everything to him.

That was normally her trigger to grab her bag and run. Instead, she took a deep breath, tried to make the decision to stay. Not to start screening his calls or blocking his number. She wasn't proud of how she usually acted when her commitment issues came a-calling—she just did what she had to do to protect herself. But she wouldn't do that to Caleb, he deserved so much better than that. So that meant hanging onto his hand as if it were a lifeline, even though he was the one who scared her, and trying to find a way to overcome her fears.

Caleb looked away then, and she had to wonder if he knew how challenging she had found that moment, but he didn't let go of her, not until they were at the restaurant, being shown to a table by the terrace, just shady enough to be comfortable in the lunchtime heat.

'So, Liv mentioned something yesterday,' Ally said, figuring that talking about *someone's* emotions was a good a start as any, even if it wasn't her own. 'She said that you'd try and push me away if I got too close and that I shouldn't let you. Just, you know, in case you were wondering about how much they all want you around.' Caleb opened his mouth to speak, but she cut him off quickly. 'She didn't mean it as a criticism,' she said, heading him off. 'She was just worried.'

'Oh, my God, why do sisters have to be so *annoying*?' Caleb said, resting his arm around her shoulder and pulling a menu towards him. Ally tipped her head up so that she could look him in the eye.

'Hey, no, I didn't tell you to make you mad. Please don't tell her I said anything. I just want you to know how much they care. That if you choose to let them in, they'll all be there for you. And not because it's an obligation or because your parents left or because they feel that they have to. But because they *love* you, and they want to see more of you. If you, you know, needed someone to talk to, I'm sure Liv would be, you know, up for that.'

'You say that like it's easy,' Caleb said with a resigned sigh, his hands tracing circles on her upper arm. 'Like I can undo the way that I've felt my whole adult life. All the damage that's already been done.'

She shook her head. 'I'm not suggesting you time travel. Or that you're not entitled to feel the way that you feel. You can't change the past. But you have a choice to make about what you want your future to look like, and if that future featured seeing a lot more of your family I think they'd be really happy about that.'

He sat with her words for a few minutes, and she wished she could guess what he was thinking. Until he spoke, and she wished that they'd stayed sitting in silence instead.

'You know the same applies to you, don't you?' he said, dropping his eyes and finally meeting her gaze head-on. His hands drifting further round her back until she was fully in the circle of his arm. 'I know that you've avoided letting people close since you were sick. That you're scared that you might hurt them by getting sick again. Or, I don't know, that you would get hurt if you had to go through what your parents did. Your folks have put a lot of pressure on you to want the same things that they want for you. But if you wanted to talk to them about it, and you wanted someone there to support you… Then we could do that.' He took a deep breath, obviously choosing his words with care. 'If you wanted things to be different in the future, with the people who care about you, they could be.'

She narrowed her eyes at him, trying to work out if he meant what she thought that he might.

'With people who care about me,' she repeated carefully. 'Are we still talking about my family here, or are we talking about us?'

His hand stilled abruptly enough that she was worried that she had got completely the wrong idea, and he had only been talking about her relationship with her parents.

'I'm talking about your family,' he said slowly. 'But I'm talking about us as well, that's if… You said yourself that this is normally when you get freaked out and leave. I really don't want that to happen. So if you want things to be different, with me, then I want to try that too.'

'Different like being together? Properly?' she asked before she could think better of the question, preoccupied with wondering how this had turned around so that they were talking about her. She wasn't sure how that had happened, or how Caleb had got such a good insight into her worst fears that sometimes it felt as if he were reading her mind. Voicing her most insidious fears. That was the only reason that she could ask him that—even hint at the possibility of them having a relationship in future. Because the way they were going, he'd be able to guess without her saying a word anyway.

Caleb gulped—with nerves, she guessed, at the bluntness of her question, the implications of which were only just beginning to sink in. She fought the urge to take the question back, too curious to know what his answer would be. To explain that she wasn't suggesting that they changed things right now, only that she wanted to know how he felt about it. And part of her wanted to see his reaction. Whether he was taking a chance on this, or whether he was going to follow his instincts and run.

'Yeah, like being together. With me. Is that…are you going to panic if we talk about this?'

She nodded, and then shook her head, and then nodded again, which was as good a representation of her feelings as anything she could manage with words right now.

She reached for his hand, and the moment her fingers were laced with his, she found the courage to be honest. 'I'm trying really, really hard not to run. But what if I do? What if, even if after this week and us both trying to mend things with our families, and you meeting my parents…? What if, even after all that, I still want to bail at the first thought of…falling for you?'

Caleb took a deep breath, because the scenario she'd just outlined was a real possibility. He had to face that. After everything that they had talked about. Everything they had shared. Everything that they had *done* together, if Ally didn't want this, if the emotional baggage that she brought to the friendship was too much to overcome—or even if she decided she didn't *want* to overcome it—he would still be her friend. He would still want her in his life. He couldn't imagine what his days would look like if she had no place in them.

'You don't owe me the things that will make me happy any more than you owe your parents the things they want for you,' he told her. 'You get to decide for yourself what your future looks like, and I'll support you either way. Even if things get hard, I'll still be here for you. Having you in my life means more to me than anything else.'

'But that's terrifying,' she admitted, gripping his hand to try and stop her own shaking. 'That I mean so much to you that you can promise me that. What if I get sick again? What if I die and you get hurt?' she asked.

He thought about it, properly, because he owed her that. 'The thing is,' he said carefully, not wanting to spook her, 'if that *did* happen, I would be devastated anyway. Whatever else happens between us. And I'm not saying that to try and hurt you, or pressure you. But you can't hold yourself responsible for how other people might feel if they lose you.'

'And if I lose you?' she asked, her voice slightly desperate. 'I've seen what grief does to a person. I don't want that to happen to me either.'

'You've seen what *love* does to a person,' he suggested gently. 'I can't tell you not to love me. All I know is that for me it's not a choice. I love you, and whether we're together or not isn't going to change that for me.'

She shook her head, clearly despairing.

'So I'm going to hurt you either way, that's what you're telling me.'

'I'm telling you that I love you, Ally,' he said, reaching out and tipping up her face so that she couldn't avoid looking at him any longer. 'And I'm telling you that what you or I decide happens next between us isn't going to change that. If I thought that cutting me out of your life would make you happy, I'd help you do it. But I don't think that that's how it works.'

'We're both so screwed up,' Ally said, resting her head in her hands. 'We'd never be able to make this work.'

'All I know is that I haven't wanted to try with anyone else,' Caleb admitted, because what more did he have to lose now? 'I want you in my life, and if you thought, even for a minute, that you would be willing to give a relationship a try, I would... I don't know. Fight tigers, or other gladiatorial feats of bravery for that relationship to be with me.'

She shook her head, trying to sort through her thoughts to get them in order so that she could share them with him. 'The thought of you with anyone else...it's unbearable,' she admitted. 'And…' She swallowed, took a deep breath. 'No, it's not fair of me to say something like that. You're my best friend and I'll support you no matter what. If you decide to keep on as you are. If you meet someone else…' She trailed off, not able to finish the thought, never mind the sentence.

'I… I can't do this, Caleb,' Ally admitted, struggling to control her breathing. 'I don't know what to do with the fact that you want all of these things and I want them too.' She pulled her hand away from him and looked at it as if it belonged to someone else. 'I'm trying so hard not to push you away right now because I know how much that would hurt you, and I'm trying so hard not to kiss you because I have never felt like this about anyone before and don't know if I can promise you the things that you deserve. I never *ever* want to hurt you, Caleb.'

'Then don't hurt me,' Caleb suggested, reaching for her hand again, as if it were just that easy.

'I'm not. I'm not going to hurt you,' she said, deciding on the spot that she wasn't going to just react. She'd spent her whole adult life doing that. Running towards the things that she wanted, and then away again the second that they scared her. For once, she was going to take a minute. Ask for the space and time that she needed to make a real choice.

'I need some time,' she said gently, watching Caleb's face carefully for his reaction. There was no hiding his disappointment, but she couldn't be sorry for it, because rushing her choice was sure to hurt him. She was either going to run because she was scared or rush into something because she was scared of losing him, and neither of those things were giving Caleb what he deserved.

She took a deep breath to calm her nerves. 'Caleb, I'm sorry, I know it's not a yes. But it's not a no either. I want to think about this, properly, before I decide if I can take this risk. Can I sleep on it? Alone?'

She could see from his face that he'd already decided that she was rejecting him, and she ached to tell him that he was wrong, but if she did that, and then decided she couldn't hope for more than friendship with him? That would be worse. She squeezed his hand.

'You're right, we should think about it,'

Caleb said at last, after a silence that had stretched too long. 'Our friendship is too valuable for us to rush into something.'

The shadows were stretching out as they made their way home. Their linked hands swung between them, somehow having become the default rather than the exception over the course of the day.

The traffic was quieter leaving the town, and with the less life-threatening experience Ally allowed her eyes to close as she contemplated the changes that had taken place since they had left the villa that morning. They hadn't made any commitments—other than to think, and to try—but somehow that decision, that commitment to herself, felt more meaningful than any she'd tried to make to another person over the years.

CHAPTER EIGHT

CALEB WOKE, ALONE, and groaned aloud. How had his body expected Ally to be there? They had only spent a few nights together, but already his arms felt empty without her.

'Space' had meant Ally sleeping in one of the spare bedrooms, and he couldn't help but think that this was it for them. Even with everything that Ally had said about wanting to take her time to make the right choice, and even with everything he had said agreeing that she was right—he didn't need time. His bed felt wrong without her in it. His body felt wrong when he wasn't touching her.

He would go back to being her friend, if that was what she wanted, because he felt too much for her to lose her from his life for ever. But there was no question about what he wanted—he wanted Ally, any and every way that he could have her. He wanted to love her as a friend and an accomplice, as a lover and as a partner. But he couldn't tell her any of that without spooking her more than she already was.

He was asking more of her than anyone she'd stuck by in a long time. She had her reasons for not wanting a relationship—and it wasn't his place to decide what was right for her. The only hope that he could cling to was that she was still here. Yes, she'd decided that 'space' meant separate beds. It would hardly have qualified if it hadn't.

But she hadn't ghosted him, hadn't told him that it was never going to happen, as he knew that she had with others when she'd got scared. Instead, she was...talking about what they were to each other. Asking for what she needed. Still trying to take tiny little baby steps towards what this might be if they both decided that they could lay their traumas to rest.

He tried to mentally prepare himself for the conversations that they would have to have if they were going to make this work. The effort that he was going to have to make with his family if he wanted to find out whether Ally was right, and he'd been wrong about his relationship with them all this time.

But what if she was right? What if his family hadn't resented needing to take care of him all this time? What if they really did want to spend time with him? If he had got that wrong…what else was he mistaken about? How much of his identity had he built on that false assumption, and what was going to be left if he decided that he had to unpick it all? Was he the same person if he realised that he'd been wrong about something so fundamental all his life?

He just hoped that he would still have Ally in his life while he tried to figure it out. That realising he could be open to someone having feelings for him didn't scare her off. Whatever realisations he'd come to about himself, he'd have to be careful about how much he showed her. Just because he was rethinking things didn't mean that she was too.

He heard noise coming from the kitchen and figured someone was up making coffee. Was it Ally? He eased himself out of the bed, slightly buzzed from nerves—what would he say to her?

'You're up,' Liv said, sounding surprised as she poured water into the coffee pot, and he deflated. 'Do you want coffee?' she asked. 'I don't think anyone else is up. Does Ally want a cup?'

'I think she's still asleep, but, yeah, I'll have one,' he said.

'Cool, come sit while it's brewing,' she said, and he hesitated for only a moment before dropping into one of the chairs by the table.

'Ally said you talked about me a couple of days ago,' he said, figuring this was one of those conversations that you just had to dive into.

Liv raised an eyebrow at him. 'Yeah, I did. Oh, God, you're not telling me this because you've gone and done something stupid like break up with her, are you?'

He huffed out a laugh. 'Thanks for the vote of confidence. But no, we've not broken up.' That much was true, though he'd be hard pressed to describe what they *were*.

'She said you'd all like it if I hung out with you more,' Caleb said, the words spoken so fast he wasn't even sure that they were intelligible.

But they must have been because Liv punched him in the arm in the way only a sister could get away with. 'Duh. We've been literally saying that to your face for a year. But when your *girlfriend* says it, you listen?'

He was about to retort when a door opened behind them and Jonathan appeared in the doorway to his and Rowan's room. 'Is there any reason you two can't squabble at a more decent hour?' he asked, rubbing at his forehead. 'Or a more reasonable volume?'

Caleb went to stand, but Liv grabbed his forearm, forcing him down into his seat. 'He's teasing,' she told Caleb with intense eye contact. 'He only sounds serious because that stick up his backside doesn't dislodge until after eight o'clock. Jonathan, Caleb is talking about his feelings. Come and sit down.'

Caleb sighed. A year ago, Liv and Jonathan couldn't be within ten feet of each other without a fight breaking out. It was one of the reasons it had been so much easier to spend time alone than with the two of them. But somehow things had got worse as their relationship had healed, and he had been the one left out as they had started to spend more time together. Jonathan did as he was told, ruffling Liv's hair affectionately on the way, and Caleb felt a pang of something like affection and something he realised was a little like jealousy.

How had they managed to sort their lives out? he wanted to know. He knew that his brother couldn't have been unaffected by their parents leaving them. And he'd had so many more responsibilities to shoulder. He should be more affected by it than anyone. And Liv—she had been closer to their parents than her brothers, and yet here she was seemingly settled and happy. She and Adam shouldn't work. From what Caleb had seen of their relationship, they spent more time arguing than not. But he couldn't deny from the way that they looked at each other that they were completely besotted. And he *knew* that Liv had had things tough. That she'd pushed people away after being abandoned. So what was the trick? he wondered. How did you get past that?

All of a sudden he felt that for the last year he'd been a spectator at a dance that he didn't understand, but now he was starting to recognise the patterns. Somehow his siblings—survivors of the same trauma as him—had come out of it unscathed, and he was the only one left floundering. Except, he knew that wasn't true. They had wounds as well, but they'd allowed theirs to heal, whereas he was still here, crouching over his protectively, not letting it see sunlight or fresh air. Not even giving himself a chance to recover.

He supposed that the sensible thing to do would be to ask Liv or Jonathan how they had managed what looked impossible from his perspective. But in order to do that he'd have to have the sort of relationship where he could talk to the people who knew him best about the pain he had lived in for so long without really feeling it—and he had ensured that that relationship could never grow as it should.

'So what's going on?' Jonathan asked, once Liv had left to retrieve the coffee, and returned with three steaming cups. 'Are we having a family meeting?'

'We're having a family meeting,' Liv agreed, and Caleb only just managed to suppress his groan. 'I'm telling Caleb that, yes, we actually meant it when we've all been trying for the past year to get him to spend more time with us.'

Jonathan nodded approvingly and pulled one of the cups of coffee towards himself. He gave Caleb what he'd once called his Disapproving Parent look. 'Of course we want you to spend more time with us,' he agreed. 'How could you doubt that?'

All of a sudden, with Jonathan looking so sincere, and Liv watching them intently, her chin resting on her hand, Caleb wasn't sure why he doubted what they were saying. Did it really make sense that they would be saying the exact opposite of what they were thinking? If he removed his emotional baggage from the picture and just took them at their word, then…he'd been wrong all this time? But he had to be sure. If they were going to make him talk about his feelings, he could at least make sure that he would leave this conversation without any doubts.

'I believe you want to see me,' Caleb said, taking his first sip of scalding-hot coffee. Tiptoeing through his words with just as much care. 'I know that you all care about me—'

'Good,' Liv interjected, punching his arm,

almost making him spill his coffee. Jonathan sighed, and Caleb took a breath, soldiering on.

'But I also know that part of the reason you care about me is because you think you have to. Mum and Dad left, and you were left in charge, Jonathan, and then our grandparents died, and we were all each other had. And I know you both think that you have to keep an eye on me because I'm the youngest. I just don't want you both feeling responsible for me. I'm an adult. This isn't—I'm not—something that you have to be burdened with indefinitely. Mum and Dad didn't consider taking care of us a life-long commitment, so I don't see why you should have to either.' He finished speaking and kept his eyes on his coffee, not able to risk seeing what his brother and sister thought of what he had said. It had all come out in a rush, gaining momentum so swiftly that he wouldn't have been able to stop if he'd wanted to.

Jonathan slowly, carefully, replaced his coffee cup on the table. 'Is that what you think, Caleb? That we want to spend time with you because we feel *responsible* for you? That you're some sort of obligation that we've been stuck with all this time?'

Caleb risked a glance up. 'Well, isn't it?' he asked, in all honesty not sure of the answer.

'No!' Liv and Jonathan cried in unison. Oh. That was…compelling. Convincing. They weren't faking their shock at his words.

'Of course you're not an *obligation*,' Liv carried on, sounding horrified. 'We want to spend time with you because we *love* you and you're *fun* and you make us *laugh*. We've all been screwed up but somehow me and Jonathan have landed two pretty amazing people who have made us happy and like hanging out with us and we just want to share that with you.'

'And if I don't want to be with someone? What if I'm always just the spare wheel, tagging along with his grown-up, married siblings?'

'That's not what Liv meant,' Jonathan said, taking his life into his hands by speaking for his sister, Caleb thought. 'Listen, Caleb—what Mum and Dad did to us…it messed us all up. How could it not? But that doesn't mean we have to stay that way. For me, it was meeting Rowan that made me see that, but it doesn't mean you have to want or have the same things that we do. We—all of us—want you in our lives. And if you also want to share that life with a partner, that's great, anyone you love is a part of our family whether they like it or not. And if you don't, we'll take you just the way you are.'

Caleb sat in silence while Jonathan's words sank in. 'I don't know what to say,' Caleb admitted eventually. 'You guys felt like this too? But it gets better?'

'It honestly does,' Liv said, topping up all of their cups. 'I know that Jonathan and Ro are gross, but letting go of what Mum and Dad did to us… It's honestly pretty great. And I got a hot beefcake of a boyfriend out of it, so there's that.'

'Hot beefcake fiancé,' Adam corrected her, appearing in the doorway. 'Is this a Kinley-only breakfast or can I have some of that coffee?'

'In a few months half of my coffee will be legally yours anyway,' Liv conceded, taking a last sip before passing him the rest of her cup. 'Adam, come tell Caleb you want to hang out with him.'

'Caleb, I want to hang out with you,' Adam said obediently, pulling out a chair and sitting beside Liv. 'What's going on?' he added, quirking a brow at Caleb. 'Am I marrying Caleb instead now?'

'Is this another one of Liv's interventions?' Rowan asked, appearing behind Jonathan and bending down to wrap her arms around him. 'Has it worked this time?'

'Looks like it might have,' Jonathan said, turning to kiss her. 'He's still here, so it's already going better than the last one.'

'You okay, Cal? They going easy on you?' Rowan asked, flashing him an understanding smile.

'Yeah, I think I am okay,' he admitted, and then scraped the legs of his chair back when he spotted Ally, still in her robe, in the doorway.

'Hey,' Caleb said, looking sleep-ruffled and pink across the bridge of his nose, sitting at the table surrounded by his family. She'd missed him last night. Had used every shred of her self-control to insist to herself that she needed to take the space that she'd asked for to think and decide on her future. But if her taking some space had led him back to her family, she couldn't be sorry for it.

'Morning,' she replied with a hesitant smile. 'Did I sleep in?' she asked, taking in the coffee cups and the whole family gathered around the table.

'Impromptu family meeting,' Liv informed her and pulled her down to the table with a hand on her arm. 'You got through to him,' she announced gleefully. 'I knew you would.'

Ally smiled back, looking over at Caleb. She wanted to reach for him, but didn't know if she could. Didn't know if she still had touching privileges after asking for space the night before.

'I didn't do anything,' Ally said, looking around her warily, her eyes snagging on Caleb's. 'You guys all love him; he was bound to work it out eventually. He's smarter than you give him credit for.'

Liv grinned, not disagreeing. 'All the same. Thank you. We like you—we're not going to let you go now, you do realise that. We sort of have a once-in-never-out rule these days. You should ask Rowan and Adam.'

'What was that?' Adam asked, breaking away from a conversation with Jonathan and coming to sit on the arm of Liv's chair and giving her something that could have been a kiss on the temple or a headlock, it was hard for a casual observer to tell.

'Nothing,' Liv protested immediately, and loudly. 'We were just telling Ally that we like her very much and we have every intention of keeping her.'

'Liv, drop it,' Caleb said, and Ally could hear the warning in his voice. Because he didn't want his sister pressuring her into a commitment? Or because he'd decided himself that this wasn't going to work and was planning on breaking up with her as soon as he found a convenient moment? Or perhaps it was just because she had asked for space and she was reading something in his words that hadn't been there.

'Well, I've enjoyed meeting you all too,' she said. 'I'd love to see you all again.' That was non-committal enough, she reasoned. She and Caleb would be friends in the future, if nothing more. She couldn't imagine that she would never meet them again.

'Well, you'll be at the wedding, of course,'

Liv said, as if that were something that had been arranged long ago.

'Um…wedding?' Ally asked.

'Mine and Adam's,' Liv said slowly, her brows drawn together. 'At the Cotswolds house, in the autumn. Don't tell me Caleb hasn't invited you, because then I would have to hurt him.'

'Liv—' Caleb said, but his sister waved him away.

'We're not making a big song and dance of it. Just close family. But we'd love you there. Wouldn't we, Adam?'

Adam looked surprised to have been consulted, but agreed with his fiancée anyway.

'Thank you, that's a real honour,' she said politely. 'Then of course I'll be there.' She forced a smile, hoping they couldn't see the strain. Even as Caleb's best friend, she'd want to be there for him at the wedding. The only real question was whether he would want her there after they'd talked about what they were going to be to each other.

'Liv, give her a break,' Caleb said with a smile that she noticed didn't quite reach his eyes. He reached for her hand and squeezed tight, and she relaxed slightly under its pressure. Whatever happened, she and Caleb would deal with it together, one way or another—she had to trust in that. She might be terrified of what came next, but at least she had her best friend with her while she did it.

'So, are you two going to be following us up the aisle?' Liv asked, and Ally froze.

'Right, that's it,' Adam said, pulling Liv off her chair and wrapping his arms around her waist, taking her off her feet. Liv squealed, only half in dismay. 'I'm sorry about my fiancée,' Adam said. 'Please ignore her completely, she's a terrible person.'

At this, Liv was so distracted in arguing with Adam that she quite forgot about interrogating Ally. Rowan and Jonathan had drifted off for a walk, talking in low tones as they took the steps from the terrace down to the shore of the lake.

And then the whole kitchen had emptied out, and Ally was left looking at Caleb, who was still sitting at the table, looking slightly shell-shocked. She gave his hand a gentle squeeze, pulling him back into the moment, and he made himself smile at her.

'Ally, I'm sorry. That was—'

'Are you okay?' she asked. 'Things okay with your family?'

'They're fine,' he said, aware that she had just dodged his question. 'Better than fine. I think we might actually be working some stuff out,' he admitted.

'I'm so pleased for you. Honestly, I know how much you mean to them, and they're so great. I mean, your sister just proposed on your behalf and everything.'

Caleb groaned, dropping his face into his hands. 'Ally, I'm so sorry she said that. I'll talk to her, honestly. I know you need space and the last thing you want is that sort of pressure.'

'It's fine,' Ally said. 'She doesn't know how things really are between us.' And, somehow, her words only added to the extreme awkwardness of the moment. 'And nor do we, yet.'

'No. I already told you, you can take as much space and as much time as you need. The only thing I'd ask is…' He hesitated, not knowing if he was doing the right thing. 'If you've decided that this isn't what you want, just tell me. Get it over with. I know that it will hurt, because even though I've tried so hard I don't think I know how to not fall in love with you. And if I'm going to have to try and get over you, I'd rather know now.'

'But you can't really be in love with me—it's only been a couple of days,' she said, surprise forcing the words out of her.

Caleb gave a strangled little laugh, hoping that it would cover how close his heart was to breaking.

'Ally,' he said gently. 'I know what I feel. It was already too late for me by the time your plane landed. It's been going on for months. You know it has. And I'm not saying this to pressure you. I'll still love you as a friend. But you deserve all the facts before you make a decision.'

'I'm still worried that I'll hurt you,' Ally said quietly, leaning in and resting her forehead on his chest, hiding her face from him. 'That you're going to pin all your hopes on me being…everything to you, and one day I won't be here. It nearly broke me, seeing how much pain love can cause. You don't deserve any more pain after everything that you've been through.'

Caleb brushed her hair back from her face, tipped it up so that she was looking him in the eye. 'You know, if it's what's on offer, I'll go back to texting, and looking forward to my phone buzzing and knowing that it's you. And I'll still want to tell you about the good stuff that happens in my day or to call you and moan when it's a bad one. And I never want to do anything that might risk me losing that. But…' He took a breath, and she hoped that it was for courage. Because they were so, so close to them both having what they wanted. All they had to do was each keep being brave, just a little at a time. 'I've seen what we might be if we trusted ourselves to have more,' Caleb went on. 'And now that I know what we could be, I don't want to let go of that. I will, if you need me to, but what I *want* is for you to be the centre of my world.'

He leaned in, risked brushing a kiss against her lips, and let out a groan when she leaned into it.

'You're the reason that knowing my family loves me doesn't make me want to lock myself in a cellar and never come out,' he told her when they broke apart. 'I had fun with them, Ally. Actual fun, and that was all because of you. I'm not asking you to love me back. I'm just asking you not to shut me out just because I love you.'

Ally tucked her head beneath his chin again. 'I'm not going to shut you out. I'm not going to walk away. I can't,' she promised him.

He kissed the top of her head and breathed out a sigh of relief. 'Thank God, Ally.' He squeezed his arms tight around her and kissed her again. 'Because I don't know how I would cope if I had to let you go.'

Their agreement not to lose one another had been so fragile that it still felt too risky to loosen his arms, to move his chin from where it rested on the top of her head, without losing the fragile equilibrium that they had just found.

He'd spent the night away from her, giving her the space she needed. But now he held on tight for fear of losing her for ever. Her arms were tight around him too, as if she knew too how precarious was the situation in which they found themselves.

Ally stirred in his arms, and he looked down at the top of her head, waiting for the moment when she would look up and meet his eyes and they would have to decide what to do next.

He loved her, but that didn't make anything certain between them. If anything, they were on shakier ground than they had been before. Even if she felt the same way, that didn't mean that she would want to commit to him.

But she hadn't run yet.

He breathed in the scent of her hair, committing it to memory. Perhaps this was just the calm before the storm, and any minute she'd be spoiling for a fight, looking for an excuse to leave.

She stood up suddenly, knocking over coffee cups. 'I'm panicking again,' she said, just as he was about to ask her what was going on.

'Okay?' Caleb replied, standing up more slowly. He wasn't quite sure what to say to that. Was he meant to hold her hand while she broke his heart? Well, at this point he probably would. He wasn't sure that he'd had much pride to begin with, and whatever he'd started with he'd sacrificed when he'd told her he loved her knowing that there was no way she would be saying it back to him.

'I'm… I don't know what I am. Help me, Caleb! I should be walking out of here but I don't want to, but I don't know how to stay either. Please. Help me. Help me stay.'

He stared at her a few moments. Because this was it. This was where they made this work or accepted that they never would. This was where he decided how much he was going to put on the line. 'I'm not going to talk you into it,' he told her firmly. Much as he might want to, this would never work if she had to be persuaded. She had to at least want to try this if it were to have any hope of lasting.

'I don't need to be talked into it,' she told him, leaning into him slightly before catching herself and putting space back between them. 'I *want* to be here, Cal. I *want* to stay. But I'm working against the best part of fifteen years of habit, here. *Please.* Don't let me mess this up. Don't let me lose you.'

He took a breath, thought quickly. She was asking him, begging him, to make this work. That wasn't the act of someone who wanted to run away, it was someone who wanted to be here, but had never done this before. Well, it wasn't as if he knew how to do this either. But maybe that was for the best. Maybe a clueless pair muddling through, trying to work it out together, was exactly what this situation needed. There was only one way that they were going to find that out.

He reset the cups on the table and mopped up the coffee. 'Right. We are not going to screw this up. I want this to work. You want this to work, so we will sit at this table with a cup of coffee each and talk about it like adults.' He marvelled that he sounded as if he knew what he was talking about. Because he didn't. He was very much making this up as he went along in the blind hope that somehow they would find the answer. All he wanted to do—all he could do—was keep taking the decisions that kept Ally in his life. He couldn't allow himself to do anything else.

'But what if I—?' He knew what she was about to say, and it drew a smile from him. Because he knew what she was most scared of, and it wasn't him. It wasn't this relationship. It was herself. It was her need to run that scared her, and at least he could reassure her about that.

'I will sit between you and the door and I will tackle you to the ground if it looks like you're going to make a run for it,' he promised her, chancing half a smile when she returned it.

'That sounds like too much fun to be a threat,' Ally said, half under her breath.

'For God's sake go and put some clothes on,' he suggested with a tortured look as her robe gaped open.

Caleb heated a tray of pastries while he waited for a new pot of coffee to brew. There was nothing more that he could do other than trust that Ally was showering and dressing just now rather than escaping out of a window. He stood staring at the stove, still no idea how they were going to rescue this. Whether it was even possible.

'So. Tell me how we do this,' Ally said, when she came back in.

He stared at her for a minute before shaking himself out of the spell that the sight of her always seemed to cause. 'You say that like I've actually done this before,' he pointed out.

'So you're as clueless as me,' Ally replied

with a sigh that told him she still wasn't convinced that this wasn't hopeless.

'I think that's been long established.'

'Fine. So we're both clueless. But let's not allow that to stop us just yet.' Ally reached past him to take the pastries from the oven and tipped them into a basket.

'I think we've mastered step one. Not running away,' Caleb said hopefully.

'Don't speak too soon. You might jinx it.'

'You still want to go?' he asked, suddenly dejected, but Ally shook her head.

'No, I don't want to. I'm not saying that the *urge* isn't still there, it's like muscle memory, you know. But I'm not giving in to it. That seems like a first step to me.'

He reached for her hand, pulled her to him and wrapped one arm around her waist as he pulled the percolator off the stove.

He pressed a kiss to her lips. 'It's more than a first step. It's everything, Ally. Because now that you've told me that it's what you want, we're doing this together. And I'm not going to let you fail. What do you think about that?'

'You won't let me leave?' she asked.

'Well, not in a kidnapping sort of way,'

Caleb said with a grimace. 'You can go any time that you want—*if* that's what you want. But you already told me that it's not. If you tell me to make you stay I'm going to do anything in my power to try and persuade you.'

'Anything…?' Ally asked with a finger trailing down his chest.

'Don't try distracting me with sex,' Caleb warned, catching her by the wrist. 'Because I promise you it will work, and we'll only find ourselves trying to have this same conversation in an hour or two. Putting it off isn't going to make it any easier.'

'Fine,' Ally said, pulling her hand back. 'If not running is step one, what's step two, if it's not sex?'

Caleb thought about it. About what he wanted after they left here. About what he wanted in their real life, rather than the fake one that they had made here.

'It's making a plan for when we get home,' he said. 'It's agreeing that we aren't going to let things go back to what they were. That I'm going to take you for dinner, Saturday night. Stay over. Eat a lazy brunch with you Sunday morning.'

'And then what? Lunch with my parents?' Ally said with enough doubt in her voice to make it sound like a threat.

Caleb forced a smile. 'Why? Because you think they'll still need convincing you're off the market?'

'No, because... Because if you're really my boyfriend, Caleb, that's what people do, isn't it?'

If he was her boyfriend? So she really was thinking about this. Committing to this. She had thought about what they were going to be to one another when they weren't here any more and the word she had come up with was 'boyfriend'. It was more than he'd ever been able to hope for. He pressed a kiss to her temple.

'Yeah, I think that's what people do. So you mean it. We're really going to do this? You're my girlfriend now. For real.' He knew it sounded juvenile, but he wasn't going to risk not being clear about this.

'If you can stop me bolting,' Ally replied, in a voice that was still too brittle to assuage his doubts.

He took both her hands in his and pulled her to him, pinning their hands between their chests. 'Please, don't talk like that,' he entreated her in a soft voice. 'Don't pretend that you don't have a choice in this. I need you to make the choice, Ally. I need you to choose *me*. Even if you're scared of it. Even if you're worried that you're going to fail. I can't spend the rest of my life—' He stopped for a moment when he realised what he had said, until he was sure that he had meant it. 'I can't spend the rest of my life worrying that I'm not going to be enough to keep you here, with me. I need to know that it's what you're choosing. I know you're half joking. That you're talking like this because it scares you to commit. Because it's easier to think of me not letting you go than you choosing to always be here. To be the centre of my world and not let that be too much for you.'

'I'm choosing you,' Ally said quietly. 'I'm choosing this. Us. I still don't know about being the centre of your world, but I want you at the centre of mine. I want to prove to you every day what a pleasure it is to love you.' She stretched up on her tiptoes and pressed a kiss to his lips. 'Because it is, Cal. It's a pleasure and a privilege to love you, and anyone who feels differently is an idiot. I'm sorry that I find this so hard. I'm sorry that the things that have happened to me have made it so hard for me to show you how much I like you. How much I love you.'

'You don't have to apologise, Ally. Don't be sorry for who you are, or your past. I wouldn't want you any different from who you are. I love you.'

'I love you too,' she said, punctuated with kisses, the coffee forgotten beside them.

'My God, can't I get a cup of coffee around here without seeing something that makes me want to stick needles in my eyes?' Liv announced from somewhere behind them, and Ally broke away with a guilty smile.

'Sorry,' she said, feeling herself blush as she held out the coffee pot to Liv as a peace offering before fixing her gaze firmly back on Caleb as colour flushed his face too.

'Never mind,' Liv said, and Ally could practically hear her rolling her eyes. 'Am I pouring coffee for you two love birds or are you going to let me drink the whole pot?'

Ally could tell from the goofy grin on Caleb's face how disgustingly happy she herself must look. But there was nothing she could do about it. Her face was aching with the force of her own smile, and there was not an inch of her body that did not scream to be pressed against Caleb. From the way that his arm was still clenched tight around her middle she didn't even need to guess that he felt the same. It was perfectly obvious.

Liv shouted to the others that breakfast was finally ready, snatching the basket of pastries and dumping them on the table.

'I guess we're having breakfast with my family, then,' Caleb said, through barely gritted teeth.

'Suck it up, little brother,' Liv said, planting a kiss on his cheek and giving Ally a one-armed hug before half jogging from the room to shout to the rest of the family that she was about to eat all their breakfasts.

Ally slid both her arms around Caleb's waist and tipped her head back to look up at him. 'You almost sound like you're going to enjoy it,' she accused with a smile.

'Well, falling in love with you must have turned me soft,' he said, leaning down to kiss her, and not bothering to break away when wolf whistles broke out behind them.

Ally finally pulled back, still half embarrassed to be caught snogging by his family, despite the googly eyes that the two other couples had been making at one another all week.

It must be the surfeit of oxytocin and all the other intoxicating love hormones that was making her grin, she told herself. That had her smiling and reaching for Caleb's hand when a week ago every rational instinct would have made her run. But, she realised, as Jonathan liberated the coffee pot from Liv and poured her a cup, and Rowan passed her the last pastry in the basket while Adam stuck another tray in the oven, and Caleb... Caleb wrapped his arm around her shoulder, pulled her into his side and pressed a kiss to the side of her head, leaning his forehead against her temple for a moment, just to soak her in. She realised that there was nowhere else in the world that she wanted to be.

CHAPTER NINE

'HEY, HAVE YOU seen my T-shirt?' Caleb asked, walking into their bedroom with just a towel wrapped around his waist.

Ally let herself look, unhurried, unapologetic. Even after three days to get used to the idea that Caleb was her boyfriend now—her real boyfriend, with no fakery involved—she couldn't quite believe that she just got to *look* at him whenever she wanted. She could just *show* him whatever she was feeling, and it didn't cause anyone to break down. It was just…fine. Better than fine. It was perfect.

'You know, the blue one with the…the thing on the front?' Caleb went on, and she registered what he was saying just a second too late.

She sidestepped quickly to block his view of her suitcase, open on the bed while they packed, but from the triumphant look on his face she was too late. He walked towards her slowly, clearly trying to hide the smile that was turning up the corners of his mouth.

It was just a little souvenir of their trip, she'd told herself as she'd tossed it on the pile of clothes that she was packing. The past days had felt like a dream, with her and Caleb finally admitting how much they wanted each other and doing everything that she had been fantasising about since she'd met him. Since before that.

But what if it was something about being here that had made everything fall into place? And what if that went missing somewhere between this villa and London. What if they got back, and everything they had worked so hard for just didn't…translate?

At least this way she would have something to remind her of how good it had been, in case her brain tried to trick her into believing it had been something less than, well…perfect.

'Ally,' he said seriously. 'Let me see in your suitcase.'

'Absolutely not,' she replied, trying to reach behind her to flip the lid closed, blocking his view with her body, subtly deepening her cleavage with some clever upper arm action to try and distract him.

He rested his hands on her hips, staring straight down at her breasts. She allowed herself a moment of victory, before he said, 'You wouldn't be trying to distract me because you don't want me to see that you have stolen my T-shirt, would you?'

'Why on earth would I need to steal your T-shirt?' she asked, with such bravado and innocence it made absolutely clear that she was lying.

'I don't know,' Caleb said, pulling her closer so that he could look over her shoulder. 'Perhaps you've got used to having me around, and you're going to miss me once we're not staying in the same place every night at the end of this week.' He pulled back to look her in the eye, obviously satisfied that it was, in fact, his blue T-shirt with the thing on the front that was sticking out of the zip of her case. Dammit. 'Perhaps you're hanging onto my T-shirt so that you can keep it under your pillow and sniff it before you go to sleep,' he suggested with a smug grin.

She snorted and deliberately wrinkled her

nose, making his lips quirk again. 'That's gross,' she told him.

'It's exactly the sort of behaviour that someone who loved their boyfriend would indulge in,' he suggested.

She tilted her head. 'Is this your way of telling me that you've stolen something of mine to take home and sni— You know what. Don't answer that. Pretend I didn't say it.'

Caleb couldn't tamp down his smile any longer, and he tightened his arms around her waist for good measure, pulling her up his body until she could kiss him without having to crick her neck.

'You're going to miss me when we get back,' he said against her lips. 'Admit it.'

She sighed. Because how had she ever stood a chance when he could just look at her and read her heart like that? Sometimes a girl needed a little dignity. 'Caleb,' she told him seriously. 'We live in the same city. You text me, like, a hundred times a day. When would I have the time to miss you?'

He bent his head and kissed the side of her neck. 'Just admit it,' he said again. 'All this can stop if you just admit you'll miss me.'

Ally sighed dramatically, letting her head fall to one side so that he could kiss up the side of her throat to her jaw. Not entirely sure why he thought that that was a threat that might work. Why on earth would she ever want this to stop?

'Fine. If you're going to miss me that much, you can take me out tomorrow night,' she said, relenting.

'Tomorrow night? Someone's keen,' Caleb said in a tone of voice that was far too smug for her liking. She planted both her hands on his chest and pushed him away, giving him the sternest look that she could manage while her body was half alight for him.

'Caleb, I have already spilt every bit of emotional drama I have going on into your lap. If the consequence is that I tell you what I really want now, you're just going to have to deal with it.'

'Tomorrow night?' he asked.

She groaned. 'Yes, tomorrow night. If, you know, that's what you want.'

He leaned in and kissed her on the lips. 'Of course I want. Stay over at mine?'

'You can't manage even the first night

home without me?' she asked, part terrified, part ridiculously excited at the thought.

'Not if I can help it.'

'Good. Then I suppose you can have this back,' she said, reaching behind her for the T-shirt. 'I'll steal another of yours to sleep in tomorrow.'

'You know what, you should keep it,' Caleb said, grinning and leaning in for another kiss. 'It looks better on you anyway.'

'You think all your T-shirts look better on me.'

'And we both know that I'm right,' Caleb said, with a smile so genuine that she couldn't help but think that he must be right.

As she leant in for another kiss she thought that maybe going back to London wasn't so bad. After all, this place boasted an infinity pool and a speedboat and a vineyard. But if London had Caleb, and an endless supply of his T-shirts to steal, she supposed she could probably live with that.

Just about for ever.

EPILOGUE

'WHAT DO YOU MEAN, Liv's gone?' Ally heard Caleb ask as she was putting the finishing touches to her hair. She poked her head out of the door of their bathroom. They'd been staying at the Cotswold manor house for a few days before Liv and Adam's wedding, and while it hadn't been the most relaxing few days—idyllic location notwithstanding—it had been so much fun to be back in the heart of the Kinley family.

'Is everything okay?' she asked, noting the concern on Rowan's face.

'I'm sorry to just barge in,' Rowan said, 'but I just went to Liv's room to see what was taking so long—because she said that she would be *right* down—and she wasn't there. The registrar is starting to get antsy.'

'When was the last time that anyone saw

her?' Caleb asked the room at large. 'And has anyone spoken to Adam?'

At that moment Jonathan burst into the room and Ally resisted the urge to sigh or laugh. Did the Kinleys know just how *dramatic* they all were?

'Where the hell is Adam?' he shouted. 'I swear to God, it doesn't matter how good a friend he is, if he leaves my little sister at the altar, I'm going to pull his guts out of his— What? What's going on?' he asked, when everyone in the room turned to look at him.

'Liv's missing too,' Rowan told him, and Jonathan rubbed at his forehead.

'So you're telling me that we're currently missing the bride *and* the groom for this wedding?' he said, with what Ally had already learned to recognise was more affection than exasperation.

'Seems that way,' Caleb said with a smirk, because it didn't take a genius to figure out what was going on here.

'Where would they have gone?' Jonathan asked.

Rowan reached for his hand and asked him, 'Does it matter? I don't think anyone's going to volunteer to go find them. We'll just have to wait until they're…done.'

'Only Liv would miss her own wedding because she couldn't wait one damn hour to have sex with the groom,' Jonathan said.

Ally grimaced, not sure whether this was the sort of family crisis where her intervention would be helpful, and then she caught sight of Caleb out of the corner of her eye. He was…pink. And getting pinker, passing through red, and onto something like…puce. She frowned.

'Right, well, if we're just going to wait,' she suggested, 'could we have our room back? I'm not quite done getting ready.'

Everyone made apologetic noises as they made their way out, and she waited until they were alone to go over to Caleb. Was he about to have a meltdown? Because even with everything that they had gone through in Italy, she had never seen him as close to losing it as he looked right now.

'Caleb, is everything o—?'

He burst into howls of laughter, so abrupt and so loud that she actually took a step away from him and checked for the nearest exit.

'I'm sorry,' he said, through choking bouts of laughter. 'I just… This family—my family—they're just—'

Ally smiled back, his laughter infectious. 'They're what?'

'They're just so ridiculous,' he said. 'All of them. Completely ridiculous,' he said again, wrapping his arms around her waist and letting his forehead drop to her shoulder as he was wracked by another bout of hysterics.

'Tell me about it. What am I getting myself into?' Ally asked, laughing too and pressing a kiss to the side of his head.

'Absolute trouble, always,' Caleb answered, muffled against her shoulder. 'You probably should have run while you could.'

She felt him smile against her shoulder, and then he lifted his head for another kiss.

She kissed him back. Enthusiastically. It was always a joy to see Caleb smile, laugh. But to see him like this, with his family, when just a few months ago he'd barely been able to stand to be around them? It was magic.

'I meant it, you know,' he said when their kiss had slowed to something sweet.

'Meant it about what?' Ally asked, still thoroughly distracted.

'About not letting you go.'

'Good. I'm not planning on it either,' she replied, seeking out his lips again, but he pulled back, out of her reach, and she wasn't ashamed to pout about it.

'I'm being serious,' he said, cupping her face with his hand until she looked at him properly. 'I want you, this, for ever. I want what Ro and Jonathan have. What Liv and Adam are about to have.'

'Caleb, are you—?'

'I want to marry you. Here. With all my family getting in the way and annoying the hell out of us. I mean, not today, or this year, if you're not ready. I'm not going to rush you. But I want us to come back here every summer and get in Rowan and Jonathan's way. And I want us all to go on holiday and annoy the hell out of each other. And I want you with me for all of it. I can't imagine a future without you in it. What do you say?'

'I say I'm in,' she replied in a whisper, stretching up on tiptoes to kiss him. 'Yes, I'll marry you. In fact, if Liv and Adam don't turn up in the next five minutes, I'll do it here and now.'

Caleb's eyes widened, and so did his grin as he leaned in for another kiss.

'You know what, that's the best idea I've heard all day, and you had some really excellent ones before we'd even got out of bed this morning. Do you want to know a secret?' he asked, after another ridiculous bout of kissing, and Ally nodded eagerly, a little dazed from lack of oxygen and the fact that she was fairly sure that she had just agreed to marry Caleb.

'I know where Liv and Adam are,' he confessed. 'Want to lock them in and steal their wedding?'

* * * * *